I'M YOUR BOOGIE MAN
A TALE OF SARDIS COUNTY

By

T. M. Bilderback

I0549594

Copyright © 2018 by T. M. Bilderback

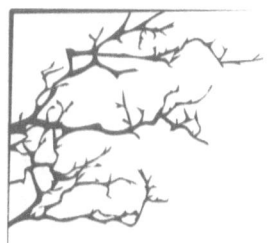

Chapter 1

The woman ran.

The school's hallway was long, and each footstep echoed loudly as she ran. Her breathing was heavy and strained.

She had been running for several minutes, and the school was huge.

The woman needed a place to hide, and she needed it quickly.

The biology lab was just ahead! She could hide there!

The woman opened the door to the lab, ducked inside, and quietly pulled the door closed. She looked around the lab, but there were no cabinets that she could hide behind. There were some lab desks, designed for two students to work together. She hid behind the farthest one, in front of a double-doored storage closet.

As the woman's breathing gradually eased, her heartbeat slowed to its normal rhythm. She listened carefully, but heard nothing. No steps betrayed the stalker...no breathing gave away a position.

The woman had heard about the Sardis Slasher the way she heard about everything in this rural place...by rumor and whispers. Things like, "My cousin heard it from her mother-in-law..." or "Somebody at Mackie's was saying that..." Unsubstantiated things.

Or so she thought.

Now, she knew better.

I've lost him! she thought.

The left closet door burst open, and the stalker jumped out. The stalker grabbed her by the hair, and then pulled her to her feet. The stalker then pulled her hair so that her face was looking up, eye to eye. Her heartbeat seemed to want to burst through her chest, and her fear was a living thing.

In a guttural, gravelly voice, the stalker said, "I'm your boogie man, honey, and you're going to turn me on!"

The Slasher then went to work.

SARDIS COUNTY SHERIFF William "Billy" Napier turned his car into the Nathaniel Sardis Community College parking lot. Several Perry city policemen, the county medical examiner, and two ambulances with paramedics had already arrived. All he had to do was follow the flashing red and blue lights to find the crime scene.

In Sardis County (*Where YOU Make The Magic!*), the county seat is Perry. Of the three official "cities" within Sardis County, Perry was the only one that had a police force. But, by decree of the county commissioners, the Sheriff was in charge of all law enforcement within the county, including the city of Perry. Billy was content to allow the Perry Police Department handle most things within the city limits, but a murder was too big for the alcoholic Chief of Police, Godfrey Malcolm.

Godfrey Malcolm was an inefficient, drunken slob. He often issued conflicting orders, and then didn't remember what orders he had given. He often told his city jail inmates to call him "God", which would have been pretentious enough, but he then grew an ego big enough to fit the nickname. It chafed Malcolm to have to answer to Napier. Napier was an honest cop, and treated everyone fairly, including prisoners. On the contrary, Malcolm often held his hand out for any stray cash that criminals may have had, and often took whatever cash city jail inmates might have in their wallets or pockets or purses, then dared them to say anything. There had been rumors of late night beatings of inmates, but no inmate had ever pressed charges, or admitted that Malcolm had anything to do with any of it.

Some did say something...to Billy. But, as the nature of cash is fleeting, Billy could never find any evidence other than the word of the person lodging the complaint. Whatever rock was sitting over the spot that Malcolm had buried his stolen treasure had not yet revealed itself to the world, but Billy was a patient man. And since the city of Perry had hired Malcolm, Billy could not fire the man, and that chafed Billy. There was little he hated more than a dishonest, brutal, drunken cop.

Billy didn't see Malcolm's car parked on campus. *Probably sleeping one off somewhere.*

Billy got out of his car and adjusted his gun belt. He closed his door and locked it. *Can't be too careful. Damned thieves are everywhere.*

Billy walked to the entrance door. Two city policemen were guarding the door.

"Morning, boys," said the sheriff, as he nodded to them.

"Good morning, Sheriff," said the two cops, almost in unison.

One of the cops opened the door for Billy.

"Thanks," said the sheriff, as he walked into the building.

As Billy walked down the long hallway, he noted how hollow his footsteps sounded. As he got closer to the scene, the sound of voices overpowered the sound of his steps. Two more cops were standing guard outside the biology lab.

"Morning, Sheriff," said one cop. The other nodded his head in greeting.

"Morning," Billy replied. He stopped just before the door. "Bad?"

The cop that had spoken nodded. "It is. Another slice and dice by the Sardis Slasher."

"Hey, none of that! I don't want the press to get wind of some nickname, especially if it came from law enforcement! You guys copy that?"

The silent cop nodded, and the other said sheepishly, "Yes, Sheriff."

"Thank you." Billy passed through the door into the biology lab.

The scene that greeted him was grotesque, but with a kind of order to it. The victim had been impaled on a series of coat hooks that were mounted on one wall, probably by the killer. Her hands had been spread out, and also impaled on the coat hooks, and her feet had been impaled onto the brick wall with a rock climbing piton. The victim's feet were bare, and had been impaled one on top of the other, so that she resembled a crucifixion. The victim's head had been duct-taped to the wall, with the tape across her forehead. Thorns had been glued or otherwise attached to the duct tape, further enhancing the crucifixion image. Her throat had been cut, and it had been obviously done across the room, next to a double-doored closet, although the amount of blood in front of the doors wasn't a lot. It appeared that once the victim had been impaled onto the coat hooks, her stomach and chest cavity had been cut open. Her internal organs had been laid out in a circular pattern on the floor. Her intestines had been shaped to form a heart that surrounded her organs. Written above her head, on the bare wall, were the words, "I'm you're bogie man." The misspelled words and bad grammar were written in what appeared to be the victim's blood. The victim's blood loss was so severe that her body appeared to be a ghostly gray. The heart, however, was missing.

The photographer that worked for the Sardis County Medical Examiner, Ted Baker, also worked as the staff photographer for the Sardis County Sentinel. Billy had long ago cautioned him about the dual role.

"Teddy, if you're going to do both jobs, you're going to have to learn to keep your mouth shut from time to time. Just because you take police photographs and photographs for the county newspaper doesn't mean that you have exclusives. Most of the time, there won't be an issue. But, once in a while, you'll be privy to information that will not be intended for the general public...until I give the say-so. Deal?"

"Deal," Ted had replied. Ted quietly kept to himself his intention that he would break that deal, if it meant that he could further his journalistic career.

Ted was now taking photos of the crime scene. The medical examiner, Kenneth Pirtle, was instructing Baker on which angles he wanted. The forensics team was waiting for the go-ahead from Pirtle, but Billy didn't have a lot of confidence in them. This was the third murder attributed to the Slasher, and the sheriff still had nothing to go on. In all three of the murders, each of the victims had been displayed in the same manner, with the organs in the center of a heart made from the victim's intestines. Most of each victim's blood had been drained almost completely, and each victim's heart had been missing.

And, in all three of the murders, the same misspelled words, written on the wall in the victim's blood.

Billy wondered if the misspelling was intentional.

Billy called to Pirtle. "Hey, Kenny!"

Pirtle acknowledged the sheriff with a wave as he told the photographer the final angles he wanted for the crime scene photos. When he was through explaining, Pirtle came over to Billy.

"Pretty grim, Billy," said Pirtle.

"I don't suppose you have anything for me yet?"

"Sure, Billy, we got a great big bag full of zilch for you. No DNA, no hair, no skin under the victim's nails, no nothing. Maybe the lab will come up with something, but if it's like the last two..." Pirtle shrugged.

Billy shook his head, with his lips pressed together. "Kenny, you have to find something for me to use. Word will circulate, and people will start wanting my head if I don't find out who's doing this."

"You don't think I know that? There has been *nothing* on a forensic level for us to give you, and I mean *nothing*. I've even had the state lab people here, and still no luck." He shook his head in disgust. "It's almost like the killer's a ghost, or something like that."

Billy kept his mouth shut. He knew only too well that it could be something magical or supernatural, but he was keeping his options open. And his mouth shut.

Billy had seen firsthand what happens when magic becomes involved, and it wasn't always pretty. His stepdaughter, Mary, and his best friend Alan's stepdaughter, Carol Grace, had some kind of mystical power about them, and Alan had married Katie Ballantine Montgomery. Katie was descended from the Sardis family, and was a witch. Her great aunt, Margo Sardis, was an equally strong witch. Katie had told Alan that Margo had sold a summoning spell to old Ricky Jackson, and that spell had summoned a Hellhound. The pentagram that restrained the Hellhound had been accidentally broken, and the Hellhound had gotten loose...and left an open doorway to Hell. According to what Margo had passed on to Katie, many residents of Hell had come through that doorway, and now made their homes in Sardis County.

And no one had seen old Ricky Jackson since.

Billy had seen Mary and Carol Grace join their powers against the gangsters from the Giambini crime family when they invaded Junior Ballantine's farm, and he was amazed that such things existed in this world...and that no one knew about it.

No one that would be believed, anyway.

But, Billy believed. He believed big time. He had to, since he lived with it.

Phoebe had insisted that Mary would take Margo Sardis' teachings on how to control the magic that resided inside of his stepdaughter and inside Carol Grace Montgomery, and Bill couldn't disagree. Mary needed to know how to keep a lid on the magic within her.

Now, it seemed he was *maybe* living with magic again...this time, in his job.

And it wasn't a good thing. Not this time. People were dying. Honest people that didn't deserve this kind of death.

As his thoughts jumped from one thing to another, Billy realized that he might as well call Alan now, and tell him to come in. He was needed.

"CAROL *Grace!* You are going to miss the bus, young lady!"

"Yes, Mom!"

"Get *down* here, young lady!"

Alan sat at the kitchen table, and smiled at his new wife's frustration.

"As sure as my name is Katie Blake, I'm going to ground that girl if we have to take her to school one more time this month!"

"Katie Blake. I sure like the sound of that name." Alan smiled. "Where did you find it, Katie?"

Katie smiled as she looked at her husband. "Some cop gave it to me. He said it wasn't being used properly, and he wanted to see if I could take care of it." She sat down at her place at the table.

"Hmmm...and *are* you taking good care of it?"

Katie smirked. "I haven't had any complaints yet."

Alan leaned over into Katie's face. "Not a single one." He began kissing her. As their tongues touched, he could taste a slight hint of the tiny piece of bacon Katie had munched as she cooked, and he could taste the peppermint flavor of toothpaste. Mostly, he tasted Katie, and they lost track of time.

"Oh, my *God*, will you two stop making out in the *kitchen?* It's so *gross!*"

Alan pulled away, and looked into Katie's eyes again.

"Well, maybe *one...*" He glanced at Carol Grace.

Carol Grace's father, Mark Montgomery, had died several years ago of a brain aneurism. He had left some insurance money, and the interest from that money had helped Katie take care of Carol Grace. But, when Katie's company had laid her off, her mind turned to the farm left to her by her Gram, or grandmother, Nebbie Ballantine. Her Grampy was named Arthur "Junior" Ballantine, and the farm was named after him. She had kept Junior's Farm all these years, and paid all taxes. It was hers free and clear. So, when the layoff happened, Katie had packed herself and Carol Grace up, and moved back to Sardis County.

After the move, Alan Blake, Katie's old high school quarterback, had moved back to Sardis County, too. His was a "have-to" case, however...he was a cop back in the city, and he had arrested the man in charge of illegal poker games for the Giambini crime family, Moses Turley, and his men, for attempted murder of himself and another cop. Mickey Giambini wanted no links to him going to trial, so he sent Turley and his men to find both cops and eliminate them. Giambini's men found Alan's partner, James Winstead, and killed him...but not before the man told the criminals that Alan might be found in Sardis County.

Alan's old friend, Sheriff Billy Napier, had also been on the Perry High School football team, and had talked Katie into giving Alan a place to hide in exchange for farmhand work.

Meanwhile, Katie had met the old witch, Margo Sardis. Margo said that Katie and Carol Grace were descended from the Sardis family, and that they held magic inside them. Katie began learning how to use her magic.

Carol Grace also was showing signs of burgeoning magic powers as well, but the powers were multiplied when she was in close proximity to her best friend and schoolmate, Mary Smalls. Mary apparently had magic inside her, too...but no one knew where it came from. Her mother, Katie's old school friend Phoebe Smalls, had no magic of her own...but no one, including Phoebe, had any inkling who Mary's father might be. Phoebe was a recovering alcoholic.

Katie and Alan fell deeply in love, and, together, rekindled the love once held by Billy Napier and Phoebe Smalls.

During a gathering of the two families, Moses Turley had taken the farmhouse through a tunnel that ran underneath the length of the farm. Carol Grace and Mary had arrived just in time to stop the Giambini criminals from killing Alan and everyone else. They had instinctively clasped hands, and seemed to be overtaken by some otherworldly power. They used mental magic to throw the bad men out of the house. Demons had been waiting outside to devour the four criminals, and the earth had opened up and swallowed the criminals' car. After that, the two girls had collapsed onto the floor, either unconscious or soundly sleeping.

The next day, a double wedding occurred. Sheriff Napier and Phoebe Smalls had gotten married, and so did Katie and Alan.

Since then, old Margo Sardis had been teaching Katie more and more about her magic, and had been teaching the two girls as well. Margo was very wary about the two girls, and didn't talk to Katie much about them...but Katie could tell that something was troubling Margo about them. Katie thought about asking her old aunt, but realized that Margo would tell her when she was ready...and not before.

Alan had already been in touch with an attorney in Perry about adopting Carol Grace. Katie had given her blessing, Carol Grace loved Alan very much, and Alan loved Carol Grace. It seemed like the thing to do.

The adoption hearing would be at the end of the month, just a week away.

Katie turned to her daughter. "Where is the 'Carol Grace approved' place to make out? Alan and I will go there, if it will make you happy."

"Ewww!" Carol Grace spooned scrambled eggs onto her plate, and topped them with a pat of butter and some pepper. She snagged a piece of toast and two slices of bacon. "Maybe out by the hog pen?" She giggled.

"I don't think so." Alan wrinkled his nose. "It smells almost as bad out there as the smell from Carol Grace's closet." He made retching noises.

Little Bit, the Boston terrier that Billy Napier had given to Carol Grace, came bounding down the stairs and into the kitchen. She barked once, and Carol Grace threw the dog a piece of bacon.

Carol Grace wolfed down her breakfast, and wiped her mouth with her napkin. She jumped up abruptly, and announced, "Gotta run. Bus'll be her in a minute." She kissed her mother's cheek and kissed the top of Alan's head. "Bye! I love you!" At the back door, she called, "Bye, Little Bit! Be a good girl!"

Little Bit barked, as if she were acknowledging the command.

The screen door on the back porch slammed hard, and Alan winced. "Having made her pronouncements, the royal herald departs."

Katie laughed.

Alan had just taken a big bite of scrambled eggs and toast when his cell phone rang. He glanced at the caller ID and said, "It's Billy." He connected the call. "Hi, Bill! I hope that Phoebe cooked you as good a breakfast as I got from Katie!"

"I don't think I could eat breakfast right now, Alan. Listen, I need you to come in."

Alan had caught the serious tone in his friend's voice, and immediately made the connection. "Another one?"

"Yeah."

"Where?"

"The community college."

"I'll be there shortly."

"Thanks, old friend."

Alan disconnected the call.

Katie had guessed from her side of the conversation that Alan had to go. "Is it another one of those murders?"

Alan met his wife's eyes. "Yes. It must be pretty bad. Billy sounded upset."

Katie nodded, but she felt a chill. "Okay. Go. But be careful, Alan."

Alan started to take another bite of eggs, but changed his mind. "I'd better not. If it turns Bill's stomach, it'll probably turn mine, too." He stood to go upstairs and change into his uniform. As he turned from the table, he saw an old woman standing behind him. He jumped, startled, and said, "Whoa!"

Katie began laughing. Hard.

Alan put his hand against his chest. The other hand was on the back of his chair.

"Jeez, Aunt Margo, did you have to sneak up on me like that?"

The old woman, Margo Sardis, laughed. Her laugh sounded like a cackle.

"Didn't sneak up on you, Alan. I just came in the back door. Must not have made enough noise."

Katie, still giggling, said, "She did, Alan. I watched her come in."

Alan, shaking his head at himself and his nervousness, reached out and hugged the old witch.

"Good morning to you, too, Aunt Margo." He released her. "Now, if you two wonderful witch ladies will excuse me, I have to go help Billy catch a killer."

"Killer?" Margo spoke abruptly. "There's been another?"

Alan nodded. "Yes, ma'am."

Margo's eyes narrowed. "You be careful, Alan Blake. This might not be a human killer."

Alan stopped in the doorway leading to the living room and stairs. "Do you know that to be true, Aunt Margo?"

The old woman shook her head. "No. But not knowing isn't from a lack of trying to figure it out. I find out something, I'll let you know right off."

Alan nodded once. "Please do. We have to stop this one fast." He started to go upstairs, stopped, and leaned back into the kitchen. "Margo?"

The old woman looked at him.

"Do you have any idea at all how many creatures from Hell came through that open doorway you told us about?"

Margo's face softened, and Alan thought he could see a tiny hint of fear there. She shook her head, and said, "God help me, Alan, I don't know. It could have been a few, or it could have been a few hundred. I just don't know."

Alan shared a glance with Katie. Then he looked back at Margo.

"I'd feel better if you'd stay here with us, Aunt Margo. It's better than you being alone in the woods, even if your house *is* camouflaged with mirrors. At least, I'd have the illusion that you'd be safer."

Margo opened her mouth to politely refuse the offer, but stopped. Finally, she said, "I'll think about it, nephew, if the offer is meant from the heart."

Alan met the old woman's eyes. "It is. Please stay." To both of them, he said, "Okay, I have to go."

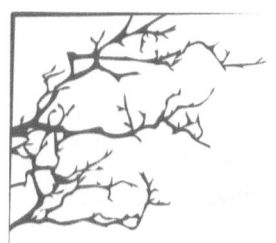

Chapter 2

Some mornings, Phoebe Smalls Napier found it really difficult to keep the kids in motion so that she could get them all safely out the door in time for her shift at Mackie's.

When Phoebe and Billy had gotten married, Billy had tried to get Phoebe to quit the cashier job at Mackie's. As the sheriff, Billy made enough money to keep the family fed, clothed, and housed. His sideline of raising Boston terriers brought in extra money, too...more than enough to support the family.

Phoebe refused to quit the job. She actually explained it to Billy, so that he wouldn't think that it was about money.

"Bill, it keeps me sane and sober. If I didn't have that job to go to, what would I do with myself on the days that you're at work and the kids are at school? I'd have all of those hours to fill...and a recovering alcoholic doesn't need time to stay alone with their thoughts. Too often, that's what makes them turn back to drinking." She hugged her husband. "So, rather than leave myself open to temptation, I'll work the job at Mackie's. It will keep me grounded, and I'm right there in town, if you ever need me."

Billy had grudgingly agreed with her.

But he had also had a talk with Martin Mackie, the grandson of the store's founder, and asked him to keep Phoebe off of weekends and only on the day shift. Martin had agreed, and everyone was happy.

Unless things turned into a total free-for-all on a weekday morning. When *that* happened, *no*-body was happy.

"*Pam!* Get off that phone and help me with the little ones!" Phoebe was trying to fry a couple of eggs for Mary.

Pamela, Phoebe's oldest, was a senior at Perry High School. Her hair was brown with blonde highlights. Her eyes were blue, almost icy blue. Her lips weren't full, but they weren't thin. She was a very pretty young woman at eighteen, and the resemblance between Pamela and her sister Mary was striking. It was almost as if Mary was a mini Pamela. Lots of people had commented on it.

Mary was the second oldest at thirteen.

Catherine, the third youngest, resembled Phoebe and the older girls, but there were distinct differences in looks that made it seem that Catherine had a different father. She was ten.

Derek, the youngest at eight, bore a slight resemblance to his mother, and to his sister Catherine.

The man that the two youngest children called 'Daddy' had been Phoebe's live-in boyfriend at the time, a meth head named John Clark. John had been at a meth lab across town, and tried some of the product that he and his no-account brother had just cooked up. It had been too strong, and both brothers had died almost instantly from an overdose.

Or so it was said. Billy had not handled the investigation. He had been on vacation at the time, and the death had fallen under city jurisdiction. That meant that Godfrey Malcolm was in charge.

That also meant that the deaths could have been anything.

The two oldest girls did not know who their fathers were.

Neither did Phoebe.

When the two oldest children were conceived, Phoebe had been passed out from drinking too much...or taking too many 'ludes...or something. She couldn't remember. And, it likely didn't really matter. Pam had been conceived during Phoebe's senior year in high school. Despite the daily heated arguments with her mother, Phoebe had won each argument, and had kept her baby.

Five years later, Mary was conceived.

The two conceptions were identical. Even though the girls were born five years apart, their birthdays were only days apart.

And Mary commanded magic.

When Mary was with Carol Grace Montgomery, Mary commanded *powerful* magic.

Pam did not command magic. At least as far as Phoebe knew.

Sometimes, when she thought about it too deeply, it struck Phoebe that the two conceptions were so much like each other, but only five years apart...sometimes it seemed as if Mary was a re-do. A rewind-and-try-it-again child.

But, if that were true, then that would mean that someone...or some*thing*...had raped Phoebe twice to try to produce a magically-gifted child.

That meant Phoebe was *chosen,* for some reason, to be the vessel for a child of magic.

And that scared her all the way down to her core.

But, this morning, her fear was twofold, and one fear was getting all four children onto the school bus.

And the other fear was the Sardis Slasher.

Billy hadn't told Phoebe much about the murders. She knew that he didn't want to worry her.

People talk, however, and speculation runs wild in small towns. And Phoebe worked at Gossip Central. Her position as a cashier at Mackie's allowed her hear all sorts of things.

Some were saying that the killer was old Ricky Jackson, the man who had been missing for some time, and whose house had burned down. Others were saying that they thought it was Margo Sardis, which Phoebe knew for a fact wasn't true. And some whispered that it might be demons, and Phoebe thought that this might be a possibility.

Whoever, or *what*ever the killer might be, Phoebe was frightened. She was frightened for her kids, she was frightened for Billy and Alan, and she was frightened for everyone that lived in Sardis County.

"Mom, I have to work tonight. Five till nine." Pam worked at the big box store that could not count anyone in Sardis County as a customer. Or, rather, anyone *from* Sardis County. Visitors to the county often shopped there, mainly because they were used to buying things from stores whose names ended with "Mart". Even though the big box store discounted everything from groceries to hardware to tires far lower than its local competitors, they couldn't lure locals into the store. The people that worked there did a lot of dusting, and a lot of pushing things around. Nobody minded working there – they'd be happy to take their money for nothing – but nobody gave any of that money back.

"I'll tell Billy to pick you up at nine," said Phoebe, putting Mary's eggs on a plate.

"I can get Jeff to bring me home."

"I'll feel better if Billy picks you up, hon. I'm not saying anything bad about Jeff, but until Billy catches this killer, I want you to wait for him." Phoebe looked at her eldest daughter. "Humor an old lady, okay?"

Pam smiled. "Okay, Mom. Tell Billy I'll be out front at nine."

Mary forked a big bite of egg into her mouth and said, "And don't forget that I'm going over to Carol Grace's this afternoon after school. Aunt Margo has more lessons for us."

"Don't talk with your mouth full, Mary. You call me when you get there, you hear? And tell Kate that we'll do something this weekend."

"Yes, ma'am."

"Mama?" said Derek.

"Yes, baby?"

"Is Catherine and me goin' to Gramma's again after school?"

"Yes, big boy, you are."

Pam nudged the two little ones, who had just finished eating. "Come on, ya little brats! Let's get outside and wait for the bus."

Mary stuffed the last bite of her eggs into her mouth and said, "Hey! Wait for me!"

"Be careful!" Phoebe called. "I love you! Don't talk with your mouth full, Mary!"

Phoebe found that she was talking to the closed front door. The children were already gone.

A feeling of dread tickled the back of her mind as she fried an egg for her own breakfast. She ate it in silence. When she had finished, she put her plate in the sink, retrieved her purse and keys, and left for work.

AS ALAN DROVE ALONG his road on the way to Perry Community College, he passed what appeared to be a huge construction site. Earth moving equipment, bulldozers, cranes, dump trucks, and men with hardhats were scattered around the twenty-acre site. It looked as if they were digging a huge hole in the ground, or had completed it already. He couldn't really tell which as he drove by.

Interesting. That's new. I was just by here three days ago, and there was nothing but a field there. I wonder what that's going to be...

He made a mental note to ask Billy later. Maybe the sheriff knew something about it.

Whatever it was, it seemed to take up a huge footprint on the field that had been there. And, because of the trees along the road, the worksite was only visible from a small area along the road, and that area was being used as a driveway to enter and exit the field.

As Alan drove farther along, he turned his thoughts again to the murders.

We need to catch this one. I hope it isn't a threat to any of us personally this time, because I don't want a repeat of the night that Moses Turley broke into the farmhouse. I don't know what power the girls possess, or whether the power possesses the girls, but I don't want to risk unleashing it again.

CLIFF ANDERSON OPENED his real estate office promptly at eight o'clock every morning, and today was no exception.

Cliff owned and operated Anderson's Realty And Auction (*Sardis County's BEST!*, screamed the sign over the door), and he commanded a staff of ten. With the exception of his secretary, no one else employed by the company would arrive before nine. Cliff enjoyed the time alone in the mornings, and he liked dealing with the early bird property buyers that sometimes arrived before nine.

Arlene Looper, Cliff's secretary, had worked for him for fifteen years. She was very good at her job. She arrived just before eight every morning to start the coffee brewing, and to set up her day.

Cliff kept a close eye on Arlene's legs. They were nice legs, and he dreamed of one day having those legs wrapped around his waist. Occasionally, he would steal a glance at Arlene's boobs, just to make sure that they were behaving the way a gorgeous woman's boobs should behave, but her legs around his waist commanded most of his daydream time. He had dreamed this dream every single day that Arlene had worked for him. Only one thing had ever kept him from pursuing that dream, and it wasn't fear of sexual harassment or a charge of inappropriate workplace behavior.

Arlene lived in London, the southernmost town in Sardis County.

Cliff was deathly afraid of London.

It wasn't anything that he could really put a finger on, either. Something about that hole-in-the-road town frightened the beejeezus out of him. He could feel his breathing speed up as he got closer to the small township, and goosebumps would jump up from his skin. Once he passed the city limits sign, his hackles would rise, and he would start sweating profusely, a nervous, smelly sweat. Cliff finally realized that he would never again go willingly to London, no matter what. Any real estate deals in London were now delegated to one of his employees.

The thought of going to London to pick Arlene up for a date, or to take her home after, was not a thought to be entertained in Cliff's head.

If Arlene was aware of the way Cliff desired her, she made no sign of it.

But...

Sometimes, when Cliff wasn't looking, Arlene would look at him. And she'd smile broadly, as if she were amused...or looking at prey.

And a yellowish sheen seemed to go across her irises then...an almost animal-like yellow sheen.

But, this morning, before Cliff had settled down at his desk for that day's ritual observance of Arlene's almost stealthy way of walking, the bell over the front door tingled, and a customer had appeared.

His customer was a petite, pretty blonde, with a light dusting of freckles across the bridge of her nose.

Cliff turned from the coffee pot with a smile on his face, and crossed the office to the woman.

"Good morning! My name's Cliff Anderson. What can I do for you this morning?"

Cliff expected the young woman to ask about apartment rentals, or perhaps an inexpensive house that could be rented for a couple of weeks. He had never seen her before, and, because of that, had pegged her as an employee of the big box store.

When she told him what she was looking for, Cliff's curiosity jumped.

"Hello. I'm looking for a farm. It has to have a minimum of a hundred acres of pasture, and a large farmhouse and barn. I'm shipping in some cattle from Carson City, Nevada, very soon, and I need a home for them. I'll be paying cash, if that will help speed up the process."

To his credit, Cliff did keep his chin from dropping all the way to his chest.

"OH, THIS IS *bad,*" said Alan. He was trying to keep his breakfast in his stomach as he looked over the murder scene.

Billy nodded. "Did you ever see anything this bad back in the city?"

Alan thought for a minute. Then, he nodded. "Once. I helped clean up a farmhouse that had been used by Esteban Fernandez. It had burned down, but there were two dead DEA guys in the basement. They had been sliced and diced. We thought it had been done by Fernandez, but the Feds clamped down on it. The scene was easily this bad."

Nothing had been removed. Billy had wanted Alan to take in the entire thing in real life, not in photos. Billy thought that he might see something that everyone had missed.

Alan took three deep breaths to calm himself. He began studying everything about the scene. Methodically, he scanned everything before he moved. When he felt ready, he slipped some paper slippers over his shoes so that he wouldn't contaminate any microscopic evidence. Gradually, he moved toward the young woman's remains. He studied the placement of each organ. He studied the shape of the Valentine heart made from her intestines. He stopped, studying it carefully. He turned back toward Billy.

"There are no breaks in the intestines. Did you notice that?"

Billy shook his head. "No."

"Look."

Alan pointed to part of the intestines. "Here's where the intestine was disconnected from the stomach." He pointed to the part of the intestine that rested next to the first part. "And this is the part that was disconnected from the bowel." He glanced at the M. E. "Am I right?"

The M. E. nodded.

"So, there was no tearing. No separation. And no twisting."

Billy was confused. "So?"

Alan looked at him. "It means that whoever did this took the intestines out bit by bit, and made the heart as they went. The intestines weren't tangled up, and they weren't torn or cut. This either took some serious concentration or some serious luck. And it took time. The two halves of the heart are identical. They aren't uneven. That would be very hard to do in light of those facts."

"What do you make of the pattern of the organs?"

Alan studied them for some time. He shook his head.

"I don't have any idea, Billy."

"Okay, who the hell decided not to call me in on a goddamn murder case?" boomed a voice from the doorway.

Both Billy and Alan turned to look at the newcomer.

It was Godfrey Malcolm, the police chief of Perry.

Billy held out his hand. "Stop right there, you idiot! If you come in here, put on some paper booties!"

"What the hell for?" bellowed Malcolm.

"So you won't contaminate the crime scene! How did you get that job, anyway? Blow some members of the City Council?"

Malcolm glared at the sheriff, but he said nothing. His eyes were very bloodshot, and his nose was a bright red from continuous drinking.

Finally, Malcolm leaned drunkenly against the door frame, barely kept his balance as he put on a pair of paper slippers, and entered the classroom.

When the police chief saw what had been done, he threw up all over the floor.

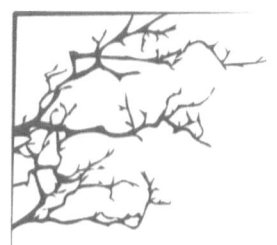

Chapter 3

"**D**o you think this will finally get the Perry City Council to fire him?" Alan sat in Billy's office as he asked the question.

"I sure as hell hope so!"

When Malcolm had thrown up on the murder scene, Billy had arrested the Chief of Police for public drunkenness. He had put the chief through the entire arrest procedure, including cavity searches...just in case Malcolm had contraband, of course.

Malcolm, for his part, realized that he had screwed up a murder scene, and was contrite...up until the cavity search.

"Nobody is putting anything up my ass!" roared Malcolm.

Several deputies restrained the police chief, and the jailer conducted the examination as instructed, and with rough enthusiasm.

The sheriff then ordered that Malcolm be put into a private cell.

Billy told him, "You'd better be glad that I'm putting you in a private cell instead of general population! Now, shut up and lay down on the cot!"

A meek and subdued Godfrey Malcolm sat down on the cell's cot.

"How long do you plan on leaving him in there, Billy?" Alan was smiling.

"Ten years!" Billy was angry.

Alan laughed out loud.

Billy looked at his old friend, and started laughing, too. "Aww, crap, probably only twenty-four hours. But, I *will* press charges. His blood alcohol level was point-one-two, and that's drunk in any state."

"KATIE, I WANT YOU AND me to try and contact some...*other* intelligences. We need to know if this killer is supernatural or human." Margo

Sardis was sitting at Kate's kitchen table. Her silver-topped cane was planted firmly between her ample legs, and her wrinkled hands were resting on top.

Katie was at the oven, putting a strawberry cake in to bake. She looked back at her aunt.

Margo Sardis was Katie Ballantine Blake's great-great aunt. Margo's sister had been Katie's great grandmother, which made Katie a Sardis...and a witch, along with Katie's daughter, Carol Grace. Katie had only recently discovered this fact, and Margo was delighted to finally share her knowledge with family members that would put the magic to good use.

"Witches are neither good nor evil," Margo had once told her. "I have a nodding acquaintance with God, and with his nemesis, too. I am simply...a witch. No more, and no less. Katie, witches are *how* they are based on their personalities...just like everyone else."

When Margo had said that they needed to contact other "intelligences", Katie wasn't sure whether Margo meant good intelligences...or bad.

"What other intelligences, Auntie?"

Margo's mouth became a grim line. "Both."

Katie turned toward Margo. "Are you sure?"

Margo nodded. "And we may need to ask...*them*."

Katie looked startled. "Are you sure we should?"

"Only if we have to. I don't want to wake that particular thing up unless we have to. But, it remains a possibility, Katie." Margo shook her head in disgust. "If only I hadn't given Ricky Jackson what he'd asked for...if I'd given him what I knew he wanted instead. Then, that door to Hell would never have been opened!"

Katie moved to the table and sat down. She placed a mug of coffee in front of each of them. "Didn't you tell me that things from Hell often made their way to our plane of existence all the time? Wouldn't they have made it here anyway?"

Margo shook her head. "Yes, they do, sweet niece. But not in such numbers! I still can't believe that I let pride blind me so badly!"

Katie patted the old woman's hand. "Water under the bridge, Auntie. Nothing we can do about it now."

Margo harrumphed. "I suppose so."

The two women sat quietly for a few moments, sipping their coffee.

In a small, eager voice, Katie asked, "What do I need for the spell to call other intelligences, Auntie?"

Margo smiled and told her.

PHOEBE WAS AN HOUR into her shift at Mackie's.

Customers were few and far between on this weekday morning. Things would pick up later on in the day, but Phoebe took advantage of this time to dust around the cash registers, stock the shopping bags, and put new impulse stock onto the shelves close to the checkout lines.

Phoebe was so deeply into her thoughts as she stocked the candy and impulse shelves, the customer that approached didn't catch her attention until he cleared his throat loudly.

Startled, Phoebe whirled around to see Tom Selleck standing in her checkout line. Or, rather, a *young* Tom Selleck.

"Oh, I'm so sorry! I was lost in thought, and didn't see you there!" said Phoebe, as she hurried to her register.

The man smiled broadly, giving her a hundred-watt smile from the gleam in his white teeth. Phoebe even thought she saw a twinkle of light reflected in them.

"No problem at all. I'm not in any hurry."

Phoebe began ringing up his purchases. "I haven't seen you around here. Passing through?"

The man smiled. "No, I'm planning to stay for a while. I'm actually looking for a reasonably priced home to buy."

Phoebe, still scanning, said, "Oh, can't help you there. We have a realtor in town – Anderson's Realty. It's a couple of blocks east of the court square."

The man nodded. "Thanks. I think one of my people might be there now."

Phoebe glanced at the numbers displayed in blue on her register. "Fifty-seven thirty-two, sir."

The man gave her three twenties, and Phoebe counted out change. As she handed it to the man, she said, "Thank you, sir. I hope we see you in Mackie's again soon!"

"I'm sure you will. Thanks again!" The man picked up his bags with one hand, and waved with the other.

Phoebe found herself wondering just who that man might be.

"DIDJA BRING IT?"

Mary Smalls was almost jumping up and down with excitement.

Carol Grace Montgomery, soon to be Carol Grace Blake, nodded. "I brought it."

"Oooo, let me see!"

The girls were between classes at Perry High School. Both were ninth-grade freshmen, and both were thirteen.

"I don't know, Mary. Maybe we should wait until lunch."

"Oh, come *on*, Carol Grace!" Mary was almost wringing her hands with excitement.

Carol Grace seemed to consider it, then, finally, she shrugged. "Why not? Probably doesn't work anyway."

The young teen reached into her book knapsack. When she removed her hand, it held a small stick, about the length and thickness of a drumstick. However, it resembled a wooden dowel more than a drumstick, since both ends were smooth.

Mary looked at the stick, almost as if she had been let down.

"That's it?"

Carol Grace nodded.

"That's the wand your Aunt Margo gave you?"

"That's it."

"Can I hold it?"

Carol Grace handed the wand to Mary.

Mary's eyes widened as she felt a strong tingle pass through her hand and arms. "Wow! This thing packs a wallop, doesn't it?"

"It does. It scared me the first time I held it, but Aunt Margo said that it reacts to the magic inside you. She said it's almost like an electric shock."

Mary nodded vigorously. "That's what I thought at first! It felt like I'd grabbed an electric fence!" She turned the wand all around as she looked at it. Then she looked at Carol Grace. "What should we do with it?"

Carol Grace gave her friend an exasperated look. "Nothing! Gyahh, Mary, you're gonna get us in trouble!"

Mary smiled slyly. "We wouldn't have to do anything *big*...just something small to see if it works."

Carol Grace shook her head. "No, Mary, remember what happened last time I used magic at school?"

"Yeah, but you didn't know you had magic then."

"Doesn't matter. I felt bad then, and I'll feel bad going against what Aunt Margo told us to do."

Mary crossed her arms, still holding the wand. As she did, she sent out a wish along the wand, unnoticed by Carol Grace. Out load, Mary said, "You're exasperating, Carol Grace!" She unfolded her arms, and gave the wand back to Carol Grace.

Carol Grace tucked the wand back into her book bag. "I know – it's the way I'm made, I guess."

I wonder if I gave Pam any powers with that wish, Mary thought to herself.

The girls went to class, chattering the entire way.

BILLY AND ALAN HAD just seated themselves in a booth at Ethel's Diner. Billy looked up just as they got seated, and waved to William Lewis, Perry's resident literary agent.

Man looks haunted, thought Billy. *Like he has no tomorrow.*

Ethel Hess, the owner of the diner, was a wrinkled, jolly woman in her seventies. She still could waitress a string of tables faster than someone fifty years younger, and she came to their table. From her tray, she placed a glass of ice water and a rolled napkin with silverware in front of both men.

"Hi, Ethel!" said Billy. "You remember my deputy, don't you?"

Ethel shifted her glasses so that she could see Alan better. "Hmmm...weren't you the quarterback when Billy played football?"

Alan smiled. "Yes, ma'am."

Ethel smiled and pointed at Alan. "You're Alan Blake. You used to come in here sometimes with some girl...I don't remember her name. But, you married Katie Ballantine, didn't you? Out at Junior's Farm?"

Alan nodded.

"Good woman, Alan. You must be a good man to have caught that one's heart."

"I try to be, ma'am."

Ethel smiled. "What can I get you gentlemen?"

The men ordered burgers and fries, and Ethel hustled the order to the kitchen.

"Billy, I'll be honest. These murders scare me. Badly."

Billy took a deep breath. "Me, too, Alan." He took a sip of water. "But we can't let anyone else know that we're scared."

The door to the diner opened, and Billy glanced at the newcomer. He was a young man in an off-the-rack suit, and his eyes briefly swept the room. Billy had the impression that the young man hadn't missed anything.

Suddenly, Billy had an insight. "Alan, why do you think the Feds would be in Perry?"

The man in the suit started toward them.

"Feds?" asked Alan. "Here?"

The man reached their table, and looked at Billy.

"Sheriff Napier?"

"That's what they call me."

The man reached into his jacket pocket, and drew out a small, leather wallet. He flipped it open, and displayed his credentials. "I'm Tory Masterson. I'm with the FBI."

Alan raised his eyebrows at Billy.

Billy held out his hand, and Tory took it. They shook.

"Nice to meet you, Agent Masterson. We're about to have some lunch...will you join us?"

Tory smiled. "No, thank you, Sheriff, I'm meeting some people here for lunch. I just wanted to introduce myself to you. I've been assigned to Sardis County."

Billy let his surprise show, as a sudden chill went down his shoulder. "Assigned? You mean that Sardis County is a big criminal hotbed?"

Tory laughed. "Oh, no, not at all! I'm actually a liaison for the government, but I'm glad to offer you my assistance as my schedule permits." He handed Billy a card. "This is my cell phone number. The other number is for the FBI office in the city. They can get a message to me, if I don't answer my cell phone."

Billy looked at the card, and tucked it into his shirt pocket. "Thanks."

"Oh, you're quite welcome, Sheriff."

The door to Ethel's opened, and three other people walked in. A young man that bore a striking resemblance to a young Tom Selleck, a pretty blonde with a sprinkle of freckles across the bridge of her nose, and a competent-looking woman in her early thirties. The man that looked like Tom Selleck saw Tory, smiled a hundred-watt smile, and waved. Tory waved back.

"There are the people I'm having lunch with. Will you please excuse me, gentlemen?" asked Tory.

"Sure," said Billy.

Tory shook hands with both Alan and Billy, and went over to the group.

"Know any of them, Alan?"

Alan studied them. Tom Selleck looked familiar, and so did the pretty blonde, but names escaped him, and he told Billy the same thing.

"I wonder if any of them have anything to do with the murders?"

Alan studied the group again. Finally, he shook his head. "I don't think so. The FBI man is legitimate, and I don't have bad feelings about the two that I almost know." Alan shrugged. "They'll come to me. Just give it time."

Billy looked up as the four new people laughed. *I really don't need FBI snooping around here with all of this magic flying around...and it's only a matter of time before he hears about the Slasher.* He shook his head. *We gotta catch this guy!*

"Hey, Billy, have you heard anything about some new building going up out toward Junior's Farm?"

"Huh?"

Alan smiled at his friend and nodded. "Yep. Big ol' place, from the looks of it. I can't figure out what it is."

Billy shook his head. "I haven't heard anything. It must be pretty hush-hush."

"I just thought it was weird. Nothing was there two-three days ago."

"*Consult the two. They have your answer.*"

The voice that spoke to Katie and Margo boomed and echoed.

This was the second entity with which they had attempted to find answers. The first entity, on the darkish side, had not spoken a word.

This entity spoke boldly and displayed no fear.

This voice belonged to someone "wearing a white hat", as Margo had put it.

"*The two shall soon become the three. Once they are three, you will fear nothing.*"

Katie, slightly afraid and a bit confused, asked, "Do you mean my daughter, Carol Grace, and her friend Mary?"

"*I do.*"

"Who is this third you're talking about? Should I keep them away from the third?"

Silence was Katie's answer.

"Aunt Margo, do they mean that this third is dangerous, or that it will help the girls understand their powers?"

Margo shook her head. "I don't know, niece. You heard the same thing I heard."

"How can we trust this entity?"

Margo cackled. "Pull your claws back in, Mama Bear! That voice belonged to someone on the good side!"

Katie crossed her arms firmly. "I don't care, Auntie. If it means danger to those two girls, this 'third' will have a fight on its hands!"

Margo shook her head. "Of that, I don't doubt, Katie. Sometimes, the good side can be as dangerous and unfeeling as the bad side. As long as their wishes are done, they don't much care what happens to those that are used." She closed the spell book that she had been consulting. "This 'third' scares me, though. Carol Grace and Mary are powerful enough on their own without adding more to it!"

Katie's lips were in a grim line. "And you don't have any idea what this 'third' might be?"

Margo shook her head. "If I did, sweet niece, you would already know."

Katie glanced at the clock on the stove. "It's lunchtime. How about a sandwich, Auntie?"

"Might as well."

"HEY, PHOEBE! YOU HAVE a phone call!"

Martin Mackie was standing in the open door of his office when he called to Phoebe.

"I'll watch the register. You can take it in my office."

Phoebe, her concern showing, said, "Thanks, Marty. Who is it?"

"It's Pam, I think."

Pam never *calls me at work,* thought Phoebe. *This can't be good...*

Phoebe closed the office door, and picked up the phone.

"Hello?"

"Mom, can you come and get me, please?"

"What's wrong, Pam?"

"I really don't want to go into it over the phone, Mom. Can you please just come and get me?"

"I...I guess so, honey. Are you sure it's nothing I can fix over the phone?"

"No. Please hurry, Mom."

"Okay, honey, I'll be there in a few minutes."

Phoebe hung up the phone, and wondered what was going on.

CLIFF ANDERSON SAT back in his office chair that afternoon. He was feeling very proud of himself.

He had sold three properties that day, and rented another.

And all three properties had been to people connected to the group that had purchased the acreage on the road to Junior's Farm.

First, the pretty blonde had made an offer on the farm he had shown her. Then, her boss had shown up, and bought a nice three-bedroom house in town. And Masterson, the FBI man, had bought the three-bedroom house with the study, just down the street from the young man that resembled Tom Selleck.

The rental had also been an employee of the young Tom Selleck-looking man. She had rented an apartment in the big complex out on the highway.

Cliff's profit on the last few days' business could keep his business running for almost three years.

And they had promised more business to come, as their employees began to trickle in.

Cliff's glee was enormous...but it was dampened, too. He couldn't tell a soul about who bought the acreage, or who these people really were.

But, Cliff had a feeling that they'd put Sardis County on the map, if their secret leaked out.

"Cliff? Are you awake?"

Cliff refocused his thoughts back into the office...and back onto Arlene's legs, where they were the most comfortable. Her legs...and the rest of her...were standing in the doorway of Cliff's office.

"Wide awake, Arlene – I was just daydreaming a little."

"Do you mind if I leave early? I have some family...issues...that have come up rather suddenly back in London."

"Oh, no, not at all, Arlene! You go on – I can handle the office! Go take care of whatever you need to take care of, and I'll see you tomorrow." Cliff made "shooing" gestures.

Arlene smiled widely...almost *too* widely.

Gosh, she has an awful lot of teeth, thought Cliff.

"Thank you, Cliff. I'll see you in the morning." Arlene turned and walked away, giving Cliff the longest view of her legs that he had had all morning.

Once Arlene was out of Cliff's sight, Cliff sighed deeply and longingly.

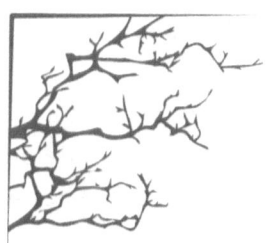

Chapter 4

"**M**om, I'm gonna *kill* that little brat!" said Pam, with force.

When Phoebe had pulled into the Perry High School student parking lot to pick Pam up, Pam was already outside. Since she was eighteen, she had signed herself out of school, with the codicil that the front office could call Phoebe and confirm that it was okay.

Pam stood on the steps in front of the doors, and she had the front collar of her shirt pulled up over the lower part of her face. She jumped into the car almost before Phoebe had completely stopped, and made her declaration.

"What brat, honey? What's wrong? And why do you have your shirt up over your face?"

Pam sighed dramatically. Deflated, she turned to her mother and lowered the shirt.

Phoebe gasped, then began laughing. She just couldn't help herself.

Pam's nose had turned into a six-inch trunk, resembling an elephant's trunk.

Pam pulled her shirt over her face again, and began crying. "It's not *funny*, Mom! I was in the middle of giving a speech in Speech Class! Everybody *laughed* at me!" She wiped her eyes with the back of her hand. "Mary's *had* it!"

Phoebe ran her hand gently along the back of her daughter's head. "Honey, you know that Mary wouldn't do something like that to you on purpose. It had to be an accident."

Pam sniffed. To Phoebe's ears it sounded a bit like a honk, but she didn't comment. "I know, Mom. It's just that it happened in class."

Phoebe began driving out of the parking lot. "Let's go out to Katie's. Maybe Miss Margo will be there, and can tell us what happened."

PIRTLE KEPT HIS VOICE even on the other end of Billy's phone. "Okay, preliminary results, if you're ready, Sheriff."

Billy pulled a yellow legal pad around and grabbed a pen. "Ready, Kenny."

"Cause of death was rapid blood loss. With the exception of the blood on the floor in front of the closet doors, the victim had no blood left inside her at all. I'm talking complete exsanguination, Billy."

Billy stared into space as Alan watched. "Again?"

"Again. Placement of the organs and the slicing open of the body happened after death. No blood of any consequence was inside any of the organs. The heart was missing. Again."

Billy wrote the word "exsanguinated" on his pad and showed it to Alan.

"So, Kenny, what could have done that?"

"No idea." Billy could hear the frustration in the Medical Examiner's voice. "I'll do my usual microscopic exams, and go over the victim inch by inch. But I'm not expecting to find anything this time, either." Pirtle sighed. "I'm sorry, Billy. I'll have a full report to you by the end of the week."

Billy nodded as he spoke. "Thanks, Kenny." He disconnected the call, and gave Alan the M. E.'s report.

Alan's face was grim. "How do you exsanguinate a body without leaving a mark? I mean, we're talking what, a gallon of blood in the average human body? A little over?"

Billy was staring at nothing. "I don't know, Alan." He stared in silence for a while longer. "I'm getting creeped out a little, you know what I mean?"

Alan nodded.

Billy met Alan's eyes. "Have you ever seen anything like this back in the city?"

Alan looked thoughtful. "A few months back, we had some odd deaths in Bohemian Village...seems like a cop died, too. The papers called them the 'Dance Murders'. After the cop died, though, I think the murders just stopped." Alan shook his head. "I don't remember anything about designs made from human organs, but the heart was missing in each victim." He thought for another few seconds. He shook his head. "That's all I remember. I can call my old boss and see what I can find out, though."

MARGO SHRUGGED HER shoulders.

"That's all I know, Phoebe. When magic is applied to someone that already *has* magic, it can cause weird things to happen."

Margo had just finished looking at Pam's elongated nose.

"Are you saying that Pam has magic, too?" asked Phoebe.

Katie's eyes widened. "What is going on, Auntie? How can that happen?"

Margo looked at the two women. "I believe Pam has a touch of magic. Given the circumstances behind her conception, I think her father had some strong magic. I think that some magic passed to Pam, but not as much as her father had hoped. And, I think Pam's father is also Mary's father."

Phoebe grabbed Katie's arm. "Katie, I was just thinking about that this morning! What if Mary was a...a *re-do*, so to speak? And that Pam didn't produce the magic that whoever made me pregnant wanted, so he...*it*...tried again."

Katie frowned. "That's just too creepy to think about, Phoebe!"

Margo shook her head slightly. "Creepy, maybe. Incorrect? I don't think so." She turned to Pam. "Pam. Let's try something. Concentrate on returning your nose back to normal. Concentrate as hard as you can."

Pam nodded. "Yes, ma'am." She closed her eyes.

As Margo, Katie, and Phoebe watched, Pam's nose slowly returned to normal.

Pam opened her eyes.

"Wow," was all that the young girl could say.

Katie looked at her aunt. "Aunt Margo, what is happening here?"

Margo looked troubled. "Sweet niece, if I knew that, I wouldn't have crazy thoughts running through my head."

Phoebe hugged her daughter. "So, this is new to all of us." A single tear ran down Phoebe's cheek. "Everyone thought I was a slut for so long...now it looks like I was raped after all."

Margo and Katie bore grim looks at this proclamation.

Pam hugged her mother tightly. "Mom, I'm sorry. I can't help but feel responsible somehow."

"Oh, baby, it's not your fault! Don't you *ever* think that!"

Margo looked at Katie. "Katie, it's time we found out exactly *who* fathered these two girls."

Katie nodded briskly. "Let's do it, Auntie."

THE PRETTY BLONDE WITH the freckles across her nose looked over her new home.

The house was a two-story, four-bedroom, three-bathroom farmhouse, with a huge kitchen/dining room, and a very large living room. It was surrounded by one hundred and twenty-five acres of pasture, with a large barn, and other outbuildings.

All she had to do now was furnish the place, and call her best friend in Carson City, and ask him to ship the cattle.

She missed Flame, the longhorn that she thought of as a pet.

Oh, well. Might as well take a look around. The basement is huge, and fully finished. More rooms down there. I need to see if I can make a panic room...if I'm not staying in the main building, once it's finished.

She went to the kitchen, and found the basement door again. As she flipped the light switch, the old incandescent bulb exploded, and the light went out.

Great. Now I need a flashlight.

She went outside to her car to get one.

CAROL GRACE AND MARY got off of the school bus at the end of Carol Grace's driveway, and began walking toward the house.

"Hey, your mom's here!" said Carol Grace.

Puzzled, Mary said, "I wonder why? She wasn't going to pick me up until after she got off work."

"Let's find out!"

Carol Grace began jogging to the house. Mary caught up to her, and they ran together to the back door.

As they burst into the kitchen, both girls began talking.

"Hi, Mom! What's going on?" said Carol Grace.

"Mom! Why are you here early?" said Mary, at the same time.

The girls came to a sudden stop as they noticed Pam was there, too.

"Pam! Why...Mom, what's going on?" said Mary, as her brows moved together.

Pam had a flash of anger cross her face. "You turned my nose into an elephant trunk, you brat! Right in the middle of my Speech Class speech!"

Mary said, "But, I *didn't!* All I did was use Carol Grace's wand to give Pam magic, too!"

Margo smiled. "That's what I though happened." To Pam, she said, "You have a touch of magic, too, Pam. Not as strong as your sister's, but you have it."

Both Carol Grace and Mary were puzzled.

"Mom, what's going on?" asked Carol Grace.

"I need to sit down," said Phoebe. She was swaying slightly.

Katie put her arm around her friend's waist and helped her to a kitchen chair. Phoebe sat, then put her head into her hands.

Katie turned to Carol Grace. "We believe that Mary's father is also Pam's father."

Mary's eyes widened. She went to her mother and hugged her.

"Mom, how can that be?" asked Carol Grace. "I don't feel the same...vibrations, I guess...from Pam that I do from Mary."

"I don't know everything about it yet, Carol Grace. Your Aunt Margo has been working on it all day. Among other things," replied Katie.

Margo spoke up. "Carol Grace, hold hands with Pam."

Carol Grace looked a little anxious. "Are you sure, Aunt Margo? You know what happens when Mary and I do that."

Margo nodded her head. "I know, child. I just want to see what happens."

Reluctantly, Carol Grace walked over to Pam.

Pam was nervous, too. "Mom? Should I?"

Phoebe looked up at her eldest daughter. "Yes, honey, I think it might help."

Pam looked at Carol Grace. "Are you ready?"

Carol Grace stammered a bit as she answered. "I-I g-guess."

They joined hands.

THE CELL BLOCK AT THE jail was actually a bit dark. The fact that the sun had gone down only added to the darkness.

Godfrey Malcolm snored quietly as he slept on his bunk. Shadows kept his cell darkened, and no one else was housed in the block that Billy had put Malcolm.

"Little pig. Little pig. Time to jiggety-jig."

Malcolm's eyes flew open at the sound of the voice.

"Wake up, little pig."

For a big man, and an alcoholic, Malcolm was able to move quickly. He swirled around and sat on the edge of the bunk.

"Who's there?" he asked brusquely. He squinted into the semi-darkness.

"I'm your boogie man, little pig."

Malcolm's eyes widened as he recognized the phrase. They widened further as the speaker stepped into the small bit of light.

Malcolm had time to say, "*You!*"

It was the only sound he had time to make.

"ALAN, YOU AND BILLY need to come to the house. Now."

"What's wrong, Katie?"

Katie hesitated. "Nothing's *wrong*, really. But you guys need to come home. We've discovered things that you need to know." She took a breath. "And we've discovered something that you need to *see*."

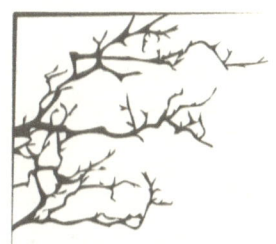

Chapter 5

Billy turned the Sheriff's cruiser into the driveway of Junior's Farm quickly and deliberately. The two men had not used lights or sirens on the way to the farm, but they had exceeded the speed limit.

They slowed slightly as they drove past the mystery construction site.

"Hmm...that thing is huge!" commented Billy. "Maybe I should try to find out what it's going to be."

Otherwise, silence accompanied the worried men until they arrived at the farm.

As they burst into the kitchen, they were met by an unusual sight.

Carol Grace and Pam were holding hands. Their heads were tilted back slightly, and their eyes had rolled back into their heads so that only the whites were visible. A visible, shimmering force bubble surrounded them, and they floated two feet off of the floor.

Mary sat quietly at the kitchen table with her mother. She was staring at her best friend and her sister. Finally, she asked, "Is that what Carol Grace and I looked like?"

Katie nodded, and realized that Mary wasn't looking at her. "Yes, except for the floating. That's new."

Billy and Alan were staring, too. Billy's eyes were wide. Outwardly, Alan's expression didn't change, but, inside, he was shocked.

Oh, my God. Pam too? thought Alan.

Billy spoke. "Miz Margo, what's going on?"

Margo Sardis took a deep breath. "Sit down, boys, and we'll tell you what we know."

STEVE BELL WAS A MOUNTAIN of a man.

He had a natural build that blended huge muscles with a tall frame. He towered over people. Steve's relaxed face looked a lot like anger, but he was one of the gentlest people in Perry.

Steve had been on the wrestling team all through high school. He won, often by pinning down his opponents with his weight. He rarely lost his temper, and never resorted to using his strength in anger.

He stood at exactly six feet.

When Steve graduated high school, he began studying for an Associate's Degree in Criminal Justice at the community college. When he had graduated at the top of his class, he used his degree to apply for the job of jailer at the Sardis County Sheriff's Office.

Sheriff Napier had taken one look at Steve, and hired him on the spot.

Steve had been a wise choice for the sheriff. Since Steve had been working, there had been no complaints of brutality, and no problems with any inmate of the jail. They all liked and respected Steve. None of them wanted any part of this man-mountain.

Tonight, Steve had Godfrey Malcolm's dinner tray in his hand. As soon as he entered the cell block, a chill ran along Steve's spine. Steve usually wasn't afraid of anything, so this feeling was unusual.

Slasher's given everyone the heebie-jeebies, I guess. Cell block sure does seem to be darker tonight. Maintenance must have put in low-wattage bulbs again. I'll have to mention it in my report.

"Hey! Godfrey! Got your dinner!"

Silence answered him.

"Godfrey! Are you awake, Chief?"

Still no answer.

He can't still be passed out. He came in this morning. Steve took a couple of steps toward Malcolm's cell. *I'm actually scared right now!*

As he approached Malcolm's cell, Steve pulled his long, black flashlight from his service belt. *Why is it so dark down here?*

One-handed, he aimed his light into Malcolm's cell.

The dinner tray clattered to the floor.

BILLY HELD PHOEBE CLOSE. "Baby, I'm so sorry. I should have known back then. I'm so sorry I never believed you."

Phoebe was sobbing quietly into Billy's shoulder. Billy gently rubbed her back as he spoke quietly to her.

Alan held Katie's hand tightly as he gazed from Carol Grace and Pam to Mary.

Margo spoke up. "Mary, I want to ask you to do something, if you want to."

Mary looked at the old witch. "You want me to reach in and hold hands with them, don't you?"

"Would you consider it?"

"Now, wait a minute, Aunt Margo," interrupted Katie. "Do we know if it's safe?"

"Yeah, I don't want Mary to be in any danger," said Billy. "Or any of the kids, for that matter."

Margo looked at Pam and Carol Grace, floating in the safety of a force bubble. Her voice sounded thoughtful and preoccupied as she answered. "I don't think any of them will be in danger. I actually think that...well, we need to see."

"See what, Aunt Margo?"

Margo turned toward Katie. "I think that Pam is an amplifier."

Alan stiffened. "An *amplifier*? Dear God, aren't they strong *enough*? Why do they need an amplifier?"

All of the adults began speaking at the same time. None of them heard Mary.

"I'll do it."

The adults continued speaking to each other, and arguing amongst themselves.

Mary quietly stood. She took three steps to the force bubble. No one noticed as her hand passed slowly into the bubble. No adult stopped her as she reached for her sister's hand. When Mary's hand touched Pam's, several things happened at once.

The adults noticed, and all but Margo yelled for Mary to stop, in one form or another. Alan actually reached for Mary, but was too late.

Mary gasped. Her head quickly turned up, and her eyes rolled back into her head until only the whites were visible. She floated off of the floor until she reached the same height as the other two girls.

The force bubble expanded with a bright blue "pop". It disappeared from the kitchen, and encompassed the entire farmhouse.

Mary, Carol Grace, and Pam opened their mouths with an unearthly scream that seemed to come from everywhere/nowhere. Each adult heard the scream inside their heads, and seemed to be made up of thousands of voices.

"Sardis witches!" The voice boomed from the mouths of Mary and Pam. "Our father will make himself known to all very soon!"

The girls' mouths closed, but they still floated above the floor.

Katie, awed by the power of the voice, asked, "Is it the third person that has been told to us?"

All three girls answered in unison. "No."

Alan asked, "Will you tell us who or what is killing people in Perry?"

The girls were silent for a moment, then the voice boomed from all three. "You are being hunted by an asuwang."

A small gasp came from Margo.

"What is an asuwang?" asked Alan.

"The Sardis witches can find the information and explain."

"Thank you."

Phoebe piped up. "Are my babies being hurt when they do this?"

The girls responded with a voice not their own. "Of course not. They are your salvation. Safety lies with the power of the three."

Margo asked, "Who is the third?"

"The third will arrive soon. The third will complete the circle. The third will give the power to stop the evil that is approaching. However, the third will not know that she *is* the third. Memory and power will be restored once the third joins with us. And when the third has joined us, the eldest will no longer be needed."

"So you can't tell us the name of the third?"

"No. The third must join us naturally. You cannot force the joining."

Billy had his own question. "Does this...asuwang...have anything to do with the new people in town? Or the new building?"

"The new people and the new building will provide more help to you than you can imagine. You must not be shy in asking for their assistance." The girls fell silent, then spoke again. "The asuwang has made a mistake. It is feeding close to home. That will be its downfall. We have told you all that we can. You must defeat the creature on your own."

The force bubble collapsed back into the girls, and they floated gently to the floor, asleep.

The adults were silent for a few beats.

Margo was the first to speak. "Billy, forgive my language, but if we're dealing with an asuwang, we're in deep shit."

Billy's phone rang.

TORY MASTERSON WAS speaking into his cell phone.

"I'm telling you, Marcus, I think the sheriff here suspects who we are."

"Have you confirmed anything?"

"Of course not."

"Good. Don't, unless you think it's necessary. I don't want to listen to Joey's bitching if word gets out."

Tory laughed. "Marcus, I don't think you'll have to worry. Has anyone heard from Brandon? Will he be joining us?"

Marcus Moore sounded annoyed. "Joey has spoken to him. Brandon is seriously considering remaining in Carson City so that he can oversee the casino."

"Oh, that's too bad."

"Tory, you guys have to keep things moving. Oh, I almost forgot! As Bureau Chief, I give you permission to accept the offer to move into the new building, once it's complete."

"Thanks, Marcus, but this lazy little place is full of charm. My wife and I just bought a house, and I think Patty bought a farm. She's having those damn cows shipped in the next day or so."

"Your choice, Tory, but it's approved by the Bureau if you want to take advantage of it. I gotta run. Keep me posted."

"Will do, Chief."

BILLY NAPIER STARED thoughtfully at the remains of Godfrey Malcolm. As much as Billy had disliked the man, he had never wished this on him.

Malcolm was hanging in a crucifixion pose on the far wall of the jail cell. The Perry Police Chief's head was leaned toward his right side. His intestines were arranged in an unbroken heart shape on the floor, with all of his internal organs placed within the boundaries of this heart. Malcolm's hands were each nailed to the wall with a railroad spike, and a spike also passed through the big man's ankles.

Written on the wall was *I'm your boogie man.*

And it's probably written in Malcolm's blood, thought Billy. *The only blood in the cell. At least the perp spelled it correctly this time.*

Alan had brought in Kenny Pirtle and Teddy Baker, along with the crime scene unit. The two men had taken one look, and both went to work in silence.

Alan, however, was on the phone, speaking quietly.

Billy continued staring at Godfrey Malcolm. *He almost looks peaceful. And he looks like he knew who killed him.* Billy shook his head. *I'm reading too much into his face. He's* dead, *Napier. Get used to it.*

"Billy?"

Billy slowly turned to Alan. His eyebrows raised questioningly.

"I spoke with my old captain back in the city. The murders in Bohemian Village were almost identical to these, except for the fact that the organs had not been displayed like these. The last known victim was a cop. His name was James William Coleman, but everyone called him Jim Bill. He was a Detective Third."

"Heart was missing in those murders?"

Alan nodded. "And no blood was found in the bodies."

"So this fucking thing killed in the city for a while, and decided to move to *our* county? Our *town*?" Billy shouted with anger. "And we're just supposed to *catch* it? How?" He pointed to Pirtle, and the general direction of the crime unit. "These guys can't find one...single...trace! How can I catch this thing without anything to go on?"

Alan tried to calm Billy. "Hold it down, Sheriff! We'll catch the person or persons responsible." Alan said this last part loud enough for the others to hear. "Billy, we have to talk to Margo as soon as we can. I think she knows what this asuwang is, and how we can catch it."

"We sure as hell can't do it right now, can we?" He gestured to Malcolm. "Right now, we have to stay here while they find nothing, right?"

"Sheriff Napier?" came a voice from the cell block hallway.

Billy turned toward the voice. "What?" he said sharply.

The mayor of Perry, Brad Tepes, was walking toward Billy and Alan. Mayor Tepes was a tall, gaunt man with hauntingly deep eyes. He wore a dark suit, almost as formal as a tuxedo, with a white shirt. He was pale, and had dark hair with gray streaks in it. The mayor spoke with a deep, melodious voice with a slight accent, but not one that could be pinpointed easily. He had handily won every time an election had been held, because all of his opponents usually dropped out of the race, with no comment as to the reason they had abandoned the pursuit of the city's highest office.

"Oh, hello, Mr. Mayor," said Billy.

"It seems as if you have been granted your wish, Sheriff. Mr. Malcolm no longer holds the position of Police Chief."

"I certainly didn't want it to happen this way, Mr. Mayor."

Tepes had been looking over the crime scene, but sharply turned his head toward Billy and almost interrupted. "But it *did*...Sheriff. I find it almost...unbelievable...that you have continually failed to capture this killer that is terrorizing our home."

"I will catch him...or her. You have my word on it, sir."

"I certainly hope that I can count on it, Sheriff. I have a town to calm and console."

The mayor glared at the lawman for a moment, and turned to walk away.

After the mayor had left, Billy turned to Alan. "Glad to see that he's all torn up about the murders."

"He's one creepy S.O.B., Billy," replied Alan.

"That he is." Billy called out to Kenny Pirtle. "Hey, Kenny, how does it look?"

"Just like the others, Bill." Pirtle shook his head. "We probably won't find anything on this one, either." He pointed at Malcolm's ankles. "Take a good shot of that, would you, Ted?" To Billy, he said, "I don't need you here right now, Billy, if you have something you need to do."

"Sheriff Napier?"

Billy turned once more toward the hallway. "Yes?"

Three people stepped into view. To Billy's surprise, it was the FBI man and two of the three people that had met him for lunch – the young Tom Selleck and the pretty blonde.

"Sheriff, I'm Agent Masterson."

"I remember, Agent. This isn't the time for pleasantries."

"No, it isn't. I wanted to offer our services to you, if you could use them." Masterson indicated the young Tom Selleck. "This is..."

"Jim Dandy!" interrupted Alan. He pointed at the pretty blonde. "And you're...Patty Ferguson." To Billy, he said, "They're from Justice Security in the city." To Patty, he said, "I almost didn't recognize you. I was one of the cops at the *Wham!* nightclub that night. You were dressed quite...differently...then."

Patty blushed slightly. "We were trying to keep Joey away from that madman. That night was a living nightmare."

Billy looked at Tory. "Is this why I suddenly have an FBI man assigned to my county?"

Tory looked around the room. "Sheriff, can we please speak somewhere a bit less...open?"

Billy gestured extravagantly toward his office outside the hallway. To Alan, he said, "You're coming, too."

Five people walked back down the cell block hallway. Just outside the hallway, Steve Bell sat in an armless chair, staring at nothing.

Billy led the way to his office, and closed the door behind them. "Please. Sit down, everyone."

And they did.

Billy moved to his comfortable chair behind the desk. "Now, it's time to come clean, Agent Masterson."

Tory smiled. "Sheriff, please call me Tory. And don't turn your nose up just because I'm FBI. Up until a short while ago, I was a Chicago cop. Jim here just recently became a partner in Justice Security, and was part of the team that brought down Senator..."

"I know who he is, and I know who Ms. Ferguson is," Billy interrupted. "My question is, why are you all here?"

Jim looked at Tory. Tory nodded.

Jim said, "Sheriff, Deputy, this *has* to be kept confidential. That means say nothing to the general public."

Alan and Billy shared a look.

Billy replied, "Agreed."

Jim took a breath. "Here goes...Joey really should be the one telling you this, but we think you need help." Jim smiled his hundred-watt smile, so bright that the light twinkled off of one of his teeth. "Ever since Justice Security went to accidental war with Esteban Fernandez, we've toyed with the idea of having a rabbit hole...a place to hide without anyone knowing or guessing where we are, on the off chance that Fernandez comes after us so badly that civilians are in greater danger than normal. A few months ago, not long after a run-in with Fernandez in Chicago, the decision was made to build a second facility. It will be identical to the Justice Security building in the city...and it's going to be here, in Sardis County."

Patty took over. "There will be at least two partners in residence at the new complex. We'll have mostly plainclothes personnel, because our uniforms are so distinct. We don't want to give away our presence any more than we have to."

"Are you both partners?" asked Alan.

Patty shook her head. "I'm not, but Jim is. I'm to be in charge of our plainclothes people. From what we've been told, we are mostly to assist your office, and the Perry City Police Department, to keep our people as busy as possible."

Jim picked up the conversation. "We intend to be good neighbors. Most of our people will live in Sardis County, and we'll be using local businesses for the building's needs. Our cafeteria, for instance, will have regular food deliveries...hopefully, from local suppliers."

Tory spoke up. "And I'm here to grease any wheels with the Bureau's influence that you might need. All on the quiet, of course...and on the cuff."

Billy's eyebrows raised. "On the cuff?"

Tory nodded. "Lab work, analysts, crime scene teams...whatever you need, I'm authorized to bring them in. Quietly. Secret."

"And that goes for everything Justice Security can provide, as well," added Jim.

Everyone was silent for a few seconds. Billy and Alan were letting this new development sink into their thoughts.

The words from the "other" earlier were running through the minds of both Sardis lawmen.

Alan spoke the question. "The new building toward my wife's farm...the one with the huge footprint. Is that yours?"

"It is," replied Jim.

Alan looked at Billy. "That's it, then. They're the ones..."

Billy interrupted. "Yes, they are." To the three guests, he said, "I have a question of my own. Please don't think we're crazy for asking." He glanced at Alan, and then looked down at his desk. He stared for some time. Finally, he nodded his head as if to confirm that he was ready to proceed. He looked at the three guests again. "Do you believe in magic? I mean, *real* magic?"

A SILVER, LATE-MODEL rental car parked in front of the Sardis County Sheriff's Office. A tall, young black man stepped out of the car. He stretched and looked around the small town. He noted the two ambulances parked near the middle of the building with lights flashing. He saw the car with "Medical Examiner" on the doors, and another car with "Sardis County Sentinel" printed on its doors.

He looked more closely, and it seemed to him that the number of cars parked in the parking lot were more than usual for a small town sheriff's office at ten o'clock at night.

An uneasy feeling crept over him, and he had a sudden chill that raised goosebumps on his arms. Patting the shoulder holster under his jacket to make certain that his Glock rested comfortably, the young man walked to the entrance.

JIM DANDY SMILED BROADLY. Tory had a puzzled look on his face.

Only Patty Ferguson remained unfazed by the question.

"Magic?" asked Tory.

"Of course!" said Jim broadly.

Patty spoke to Tory. "Hold on, Tory. Don't be so quick to dismiss magic. Have either of you ever heard Louie's Christmas Eve story?"

"I have," said Jim. "And I have met the little girl that Megan spoke about."

"How?"

"Well...just trust me on this, okay? You were still in Carson City."

Tory said, "But Louie's Christmas story was a religious event!"

"And a religious event is, by definition, supernatural. Magic, if you prefer." Patty stood. "And I would like to hear Sheriff Napier's story, and help him, no matter what the reason behind it. I only wish that Brandon was here, too."

Someone knocked on Billy's door.

"Come in!"

A deputy opened the door and said, "Someone here to see Miss Ferguson and Mr. Dandy, Sheriff."

Billy looked at Patty. She nodded, and Jim said, "Fine by me."

"Send them in, John," said Billy.

Deputy John stepped out, and the young black man stepped in.

Patty's eyes widened. "*Brandon!*" She launched herself into the young man's arms and hugged him fiercely.

Jim and Tory both stood. Jim smiled another hundred-watt smile, and Tory grinned.

Jim held out his hand and said, "Glad to see you, Brandon! Are you staying?"

Brandon King shook Jim's hand. "Yes, sir, I think I am. I've left the casino under Mark Brown's care. I think he'll do great."

Tory spoke up. "Welcome aboard, Brandon."

Keeping an arm around her friend's waist, Patty turned to Billy and Alan. "Gentlemen, I'm sorry. This is my best friend since we were kids – Brandon

King. He works for Justice Security, too. Brandon, this is Sheriff Billy Napier and Chief Deputy Alan Blake."

Brandon stood as straight as he could with Patty's arm clinging to him. "Brandon King, gentlemen. It's a pleasure to meet you."

Both Alan and Billy nodded to the young man.

Jim spoke. "Brandon, we've offered our services to the sheriff, and we've explained why we're here. There's been a series of murders in town. We want to be good neighbors. But, the sheriff has a question for us."

"Yes, sir?" Brandon looked at Billy.

Billy sighed. "Do you believe in magic? The supernatural?"

Brandon shrugged one shoulder. "Of course. A man can't believe in God without believing in the other place. Too much history has happened that can't be explained any other way."

Jim smiled his hundred-watt smile, and Tory was stunned.

Billy and Alan smiled.

"Sit down, people, and Alan and I will tell you everything that we can," said Billy.

AFTER THE MEN LEFT, Margo, Phoebe, and Katie took the still-sleeping girls to the living room. They put Pam on the couch, Mary on the love seat, and Carol Grace in Alan's huge recliner. Katie got blankets, and the women covered the girls.

With a worried look, Katie said, "I think coffee and food are in order."

Phoebe had the same worried look. "I'll help, Katie."

The women went to the kitchen. Margo sat at the kitchen table while Katie made coffee and Phoebe began pulling food from the refrigerator.

"I suppose you two want me to explain what an asuwang is," said Margo.

"Please," said Katie. "It might take our minds off of the girls."

"Among other things," added Phoebe.

Margo sighed. "I'm sorry, Phoebe, but I don't know any more than you do about them. I can't even guess who might be their father. And I'm sorry this has happened to you. But, I give you my word, as a witch and as a Sardis, we will find out." Her voice grew stronger and harsher. "And there will be retribution." She banged her fist on the kitchen table, and blue sparks scattered brightly through the kitchen.

Katie's voice was rough. "Yes, Phoebe, there *will* be retribution. We've been robbed of years of friendship, you've had your innocence taken without your permission, and this situation threatens our *children!*" Streaks of solid blue power began moving up and down Katie's arms. Her head had a bright blue circle of power around it...almost in the shape of a halo. Streaks occasionally travelled from her arms to her halo. Her face was dark with anger.

Katie, at that moment, was frightening. "So you can *bet* that there will be a reckoning! A true *Sardis* reckoning! And may God have mercy on whoever is behind this!"

"Dear," said Margo calmly. "What if God *is* the one behind this?"

Katie's eyes whirled around to face her aunt. "Then God will taste my anger!"

Margo abruptly stood. "Bold words, child! And wrong! You can't challenge God! You can't challenge the Devil, either! You are merely a witch, Katie. You're powerful – maybe more powerful than me – but you can't challenge those two! You'll lose *every* time!"

Katie smiled. "We'll see, won't we, Auntie?"

"*STOP IT! BOTH OF YOU!*"

Phoebe's scream made both witches jump. Katie's blue power died. Both witches turned to Phoebe, incredulous.

"I don't care who's behind any of this! I just want it to be over, so that my children can have a relatively normal life. I'm grateful to both of you for what you've done for us, and for helping Billy and I get together, but please remember that this is about protecting our girls. If we need the magic they have from time to time, then we'll take what we need, and be grateful that we have it. But arguing with ourselves is *not* the way to solve any of these problems!" Phoebe turned to Katie. "And, Katie, who do you think you are, challenging God? We have to *pray* that he's got our backs through this! You should be ashamed of yourself, witch or not!"

Silence filled the kitchen. No one looked at the others.

Finally, Katie broke the silence. "You're right, Phoebe. I'm sorry. I let myself get carried away."

Margo smiled. "Seems to run in the family."

Phoebe took a deep breath. "Now, Margo, will you please tell us about this asu...asa...assholio thing?"

After the mispronunciation sank in, all three women burst out laughing.

Margo began coughing from laughing so hard. When she finally had herself under control, she said, "Asuwang, Phoebe. It's a shapeshifter. It only feeds at night. Some have been known to eat unborn human fetuses that can be sucked out with a long proboscis. Most, however, use that proboscis to suck out their victim's blood, draining it completely. Then, while some of them eat livers, most of them eat hearts."

"So, they change at night and drink blood. Are they vampires?"

Margo shook her head. "No, although things like garlic and crosses can repel them. And sunlight doesn't hurt them at all. In the daytime, they look just like human beings. At night, they can change into various things, but they can look human then, too. That's why they're so dangerous...they're very hard to find." She paused for a moment. "It could be anyone in town. And, at night, their strength is tremendous. During the day, not so much."

Little Bit hopped down the stairs and looked from the kitchen to the living room. She turned, went into the living room, and jumped into the recliner beside Carol Grace. After circling three times, she settled down, and curved herself to fit into the hollow created from Carol Grace's knees curling toward her chest. The dog tried to keep her eyes on the kitchen, but she couldn't keep them open. Within a few seconds, she was sleeping as deeply as Carol Grace.

"I want to know who these new people are," said Katie.

"I want to know who the 'third' is," said Phoebe.

Margo smiled at the two younger women. "And I want dinner. Let's get to work, girls!"

TORY MASTERSON WONDERED what he had gotten himself into.

Tory was very glad he had left the Chicago police force and joined the FBI, at Marcus Moore's invitation. Tory had gotten through Quantico, the FBI's training facility, with very high marks. He had been delighted to find out that he would be working with Marcus as one of the FBI's liaison to Justice Security.

When Tory found out that Marcus wanted him to head up the backup Justice Security team in Sardis County, he was still excited. The job still offered action and plenty of work.

Tory was not excited to find out that the second facility was right in the middle of a place that had magic as an everyday occurrence. He did not delight in the fact that a doorway to Hell had been opened here, and had been left open for many hours. And the idea that actual demons and creatures of Hell might be wandering through the area didn't encourage ideas of advancement in the FBI. And witches? Well, that was where he drew the line.

Tory thought that the sheriff's conclusion that a shapeshifting monster was killing people in Sardis County was unbelievable.

Tory felt that these people had a screw loose.

Tory made a conscious decision to deny the existence of these things.

"Sheriff," said Tory. "Do you truly believe in these things, or are you just pulling the leg of the FBI guy?"

Jim Dandy turned to Tory with wide eyes. "Tory!"

Patty said, "Tory, you should apologize! That's rude!"

Brandon followed with, "Uncool, Tory."

Tory shrugged. "Hey, you guys can believe these fairy tales if you want to. But, I can tell you this: The FBI doesn't believe in witches or magic."

Billy Napier and Alan Blake sat smugly, watching the exchange.

Jim said quietly, "So explain Nicholas Turner's daughter. You met her."

Tory tried to speak, but couldn't. Finally, his mouth snapped shut, and he crossed his arms.

Billy said, "I can back all of this up, if you'd all like to follow me to Junior's Farm."

MARGO STOPPED SETTING the table. She stared at a plate for quite some time, until Katie asked what was wrong.

Margo shook her elderly head. "Nothing. But we need more food. We're about to have company."

THE ASUWANG WAS HUNGRY again.

It had just finished a meal of Godfrey Malcolm. It shouldn't be hungry so soon afterwards.

But, there it was – that gnawing feeling inside its stomach. The feeling that its stomach was empty, and had always *been* empty, had come crashing back.

There was no way it could feed again this soon. It would have to wait until the next day.

But it was so *hungry!*

Pregnancy was always unpredictable.

"KATIE, I'M SORRY WE'VE all intruded," said Billy, after they had arrived at Junior's Farm.

"There's been another murder, hasn't there?" said Margo with abruptness.

Alan nodded. "Yes, Aunt Margo. It was Godfrey Malcolm."

Phoebe gasped. "Really? Malcolm?"

Billy nodded as he put an arm around his wife.

"He just came into Mackie's yesterday!"

Margo said, "Had it coming. I don't like to say it, but he had it coming. If it wasn't this asuwang, it would have been something else. At least, this way, he didn't take anyone with his drunken self."

"Auntie!" exclaimed Katie.

Margo shot her niece a look. "You just don't know, Katie. He could be a real terror when he was drunk."

Alan interrupted. "May I introduce our guests?"

Katie was embarrassed. "I'm so sorry! Please forgive my rudeness!"

Jim Dandy turned on his hundred-watt-smile. "Nothing to apologize for, ma'am." He gestured, one by one. "This is Patty Ferguson, Brandon King, and Tory Masterson. I'm Jim Dandy. We're with Justice Security, and Tory is one of our FBI liaisons. We're building the new building down the road here."

Patty said, "You mentioned an asuwang. May I ask what that is?"

"I've actually heard of them, but I thought they were mostly in Asia," added Brandon.

"Oh, children, sit down. We'll explain it all to you," said Margo. "And maybe the three sleeping beauties will wake up shortly and join us."

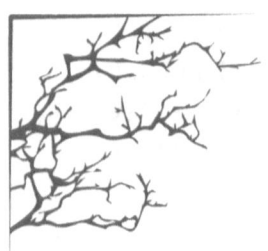

Chapter 6

The clock ticked over to midnight.

As Tory gulped the last of his sandwich, his eyes flicked around the dining room table as the conversation traveled. Margo Sardis explained a great many things about the murders that an up-to-date, modern FBI man shouldn't believe, much less Chelsea Masterson's cop kid from the east side of Chicago.

But, Tory *did* believe.

Pretending not to believe was a defensive thing...he didn't want to appear to be a superstitious idiot.

Tory found that it was easy to believe when he had seen an angel in action.

During the meal, Jim's phone rang. Jim glanced at the caller ID.

"Please excuse me. I have to take this." He stood. As he headed for the front porch, Jim answered the phone, and everyone could hear him say, "Hi, Joey. Did you find the kids in time?"

Alan turned to the Justice Security group. "Have you found places to live?"

Tory nodded as he spoke. "We have, thank you, Alan. Some of us will be living inside the new building as soon as it's livable. But, Patty bought a farm today."

Katie smiled. "That's great, Patty! Are you a farm girl?"

Patty laughed. "No. The outdoors and I don't get along very well. But, while I was recently in Carson City with Brandon, I...well...inherited a herd of longhorn cattle. They're all pets, especially Flame. So, I needed some acreage...and a barn."

Billy looked surprised. "Wow. Private security must pay very well!"

Patty shared a look at Brandon before she answered. "Brandon and I inherited a hotel and casino in Carson City...along with quite an estate. We can afford it."

"And you still choose to work?" asked Alan.

Brandon answered, "Justice Security's people are our friends. They've looked out for us from the beginning. The least we can do is help out when we can."

Jim chose that moment to come inside. His face was grim. "Joey said that the children are safe. But, there are...consequences...that we need to talk about. Privately."

Tory said, "Should we leave now?"

Jim considered, then nodded. "I think so. We know what the Sheriff knows about the killings." He looked at Billy. "Sheriff, don't hesitate. Call one or all of us, and we'll be glad to help you in any way we can." He looked at Alan, then at Katie. "Thank you for your hospitality...and for dinner. Sorry to inconvenience you."

Katie smiled at Jim. "No inconvenience, Jim. We were glad to have you folks. Come back anytime." To Patty, Katie said, "And if you need help with decorating, or the farm, or anything else, you call us. Phoebe and I would welcome another member of our pack."

Patty smiled. "I will. Thank you."

"And welcome to Sardis County," added Margo.

Brandon nodded and smiled at his hosts, as did Tory.

The group left.

THE JUSTICE SECURITY group talked as they rode in Tory's car.

"What happened, Jim?" asked Tory.

Jim shook his head. "It's unbelievable. Joey accidentally blew the kidnappers up before he found out where the kids were stashed."

"What?" Brandon was incredulous.

Jim nodded. "It looked grim for a while, but he had this cockeyed idea of getting Madeline to take them to Hell to ask the kidnappers about the children."

"Madeline is Nicholas Turner's daughter, right? The half-angel that you told us about?" asked Patty.

"Yes, she is. Against her better judgement, Madeline did what Joey asked. They found the lead kidnapper and retrieved the information about the children. But there was a huge cost." Jim took a deep breath. "Madeline got hit with a bolt of bad energy and almost died, and Megan got carried off by a demon. They couldn't go after her. She's gone."

"Oh, my God!" said Brandon.

"That's terrible!" added Patty. "How is Dexter?"

"He's heartbroken, as you would expect." He paused. "And Madeline has forgotten that she's half-angel."

PAM WAS AWARE OF VOICES before she woke up completely. She woke slowly, and her head pounded like never before. Her head felt as if she had a migraine. She had had a migraine once before, and it pounded the inside of her head, too...just like now.

Pam sat up slowly, her hand to her forehead. She didn't open her eyes yet, because she was afraid that light would make her head worse.

The young woman remembered it all.

The power that had coursed through Pam had jolted her like nothing she had ever experienced. It was overpowering. It took her over, and pushed her out of the way inside her mind, leaving her helpless as she first channeled and amplified the power from Carol Grace, then the even stronger power when Mary joined hands with them.

Power hangovers feel just like migraines. Gotta remember to tell Mom that.

Slowly, Pam cracked her eyes. The light didn't seem to bother her, so she opened them wide.

Margo Sardis was sitting in a kitchen chair directly in front of her. Pam jumped slightly, startled.

Margo smiled. "Hello, child. Did you have a nice sleep?"

Pam smiled back slightly. "Sort of...feels like someone is pounding the inside of my head with a sledgehammer."

Margo nodded. "Power hangover." She caught Pam's eyes. "But you knew what it was already, didn't you?"

Puzzled, Pam realized that she *had* known. But she didn't recall ever hearing the phrase. She nodded.

"You're either a bit psychic, or the power tells you things inside your head. The pain will fade soon."

Gently, Pam shook her head with a small back-and-forth motion. "Miss Margo, what is going on?"

"Oh, child, if I knew all the answers, I would be the wisest old woman in the world!" Margo reached over and took Pam's hand. "But I do know this, Pam: you have magic. You need to know how to use it...control it. You need to start coming to my magic classes with your sister. I'll help you, and guide you."

Pam nodded. "What time is it?"

Margo smiled. "It's eight-thirty in the morning, Pam. You three slept the night away."

"Eight-thirty? I'll be late for work!"

"No, you won't, sweetheart." Phoebe had walked into the room. "I had no idea what time you would wake up, so Billy went by the box store, and told them that you couldn't come in today. You're good there. Take today and rest." She sat down beside her eldest daughter, and put an arm around her. "You need it."

"Mom, did we spend the night here?"

"Yes, we did."

Katie came in. "And we were glad to have you, Pam. You're all always welcome here."

Pam smiled.

Little Bit began barking, heralding the arrival from outside of Mary and Carol Grace. The two girls came into the house chattering while Little Bit scampered around them, barking her joy for all to hear. The screen door on the front porch slammed, and Pam jumped.

"Girls! Would you mind waiting for another day to break the house?" called Katie.

Carol Grace smiled slightly. "Sorry, Mom."

The younger girls noticed Pam. Both ran over to the couch, talking to her at the same time.

"Pam, how do you feel?" asked Carol Grace.

"About time you woke up!" said Mary.

"Wasn't yesterday *awesome?*"

"Who knew older sisters were good for something besides bossing kids around?"

Pam started laughing. She felt better.

Katie handed Pam a mug of coffee with cream.

"Oh, thank you, Miss Katie! It's *just* what I need!" She took the coffee gratefully, and took a large sip. "Oh, that's *good!*" Her headache began to fade. She leaned back against the back of the couch.

Margo asked, "What do you remember, child?"

Pam shook her head. "Everything. I mean, everything!" She smiled slightly and looked up at the old witch. "Miss Margo, even when my eyes were rolled back, I could see everything around me. One part of me was amazed at it, and one part of me accepted it as something that was normal. Oh, and a small part of me was afraid."

"That's how Mary and I feel when we connect," said Carol Grace.

"Yeah, Pam, we know *everything* that's going on around us," added Mary.

"And then some," said Carol Grace.

Pam looked around her. Katie, Margo, Carol Grace, Mary, and her mom were all watching her as she sipped her coffee.

They must think I'm going to grow another head, thought Pam. Then something occurred to her. *I'm going to try something.*

Pam reached out with her mind. She could feel the coffee mug with her thoughts. She wrapped them around the mug, and used her thoughts to lift the half-empty mug. The mug rose from her hands.

Oh, my God, I'm doing it!

Pam gently pushed the mug toward the coffee table, where she sat it down. Not a drop was spilled, and there was no sloshing.

The other five were staring at the mug with astonishment.

"Miss Margo, do you think I can learn, too?" asked Pam quietly.

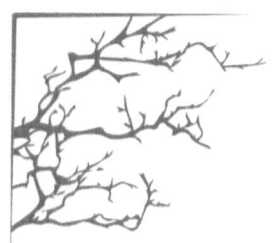

Chapter 7

Kenny Pirtle sat in the visitors' chair across from Sheriff Napier. Alan Blake sat in a chair to the side of the desk.

"I'm telling you, Billy, I'm stumped," said Pirtle. "I have nothing. I've examined every inch of Godfrey Malcolm's body with magnifying glasses, microscopes, and any other method I could think of. No trace of anything. It's as if he were killed by a ghost."

Billy snorted. "You aren't too far from the truth, Kenny."

Pirtle wrinkled his brows. "Don't tease an old medical examiner, Billy. What are you talking about?"

Billy seemed to consider. He glanced at Alan.

Alan nodded discreetly.

Billy took a deep breath and let it out slowly. "Kenny. Have you noticed anything...unusual...in Sardis County the last few months?"

Pirtle tilted his head. "Unusual? How do you mean?"

"Well..."

"I mean, Sardis County has *always* had weird happenings, right?" asked Pirtle. "After all, we have our resident witch...and there's something about London that raises hackles on some people. William Lewis was found dead of a heart attack, but he had no history of heart problems. Raymond Hollingsworth has been smiling like the cat that ate the canary...and his vocabulary has improved tremendously. " He leaned back into his chair. "I suppose, now that I think about it, things *have* been weirder lately...ever since old Ricky Jackson disappeared."

Billy nodded. "Kenny, we've known each other since junior high. Alan and I are going to fill you in on what we think is going on, and what's killing people." He shook his head and smiled. "You'll probably throw us in the loony bin."

Kenny smiled back. "You might be surprised, guys."

THE PHONE'S INCESSANT ringing finally roused Patty from sleep. She reached for the phone on the motel's nightstand, but she knocked it into the floor before she could answer it.

Chuckling came from the second bed. Patty glared in that direction.

Brandon was awake, watching her fumble with the phone.

Patty flipped her middle finger at Brandon before she retrieved her phone. "Hello?"

"Patty Ferguson?"

"Yes?"

"This is Joe Mills. I'm driving the lead truck. There are four other trucks following me. We've got your cattle. Where do we meet you?"

"Where are you?"

"We're parked on the square in Perry. We're all having breakfast in a diner called *Ethel's.*"

Patty smiled. Ethel's Diner was three doors down from the motel.

"I'll be there in half an hour." She hung up. To Brandon, she said, "I suppose you've already showered."

"Yep."

Patty shook her head. "Ass."

Thirty minutes later, Patty and Brandon walked through the door of Ethel's. Patty spotted the drivers immediately. They were grouped around a table in the middle of the diner, laughing over coffee.

Brandon had already met them in Carson City. He had paid them well to deliver the cattle safely.

Ten minutes later, with a cup of Ethel's strong coffee in her hand, Patty led the way to the new farm.

"JOEY, THERE ARE SOME things going on here that we weren't expecting."

Jim Dandy was speaking on his cell phone. The conversation was with Joey Justice.

Seated at Jim's home desk, watching him and listening to his side of the conversation, was Emily Owens. Emily had been Jim's executive assistant before they had joined Justice Security, and she would be performing the executive secretary duties in the new facility. Her boyfriend, Turk Wendell, performed the same duties at the main branch of Justice Security.

"What kind of things, Jim?"

"Well...the sheriff has had a series of murders here, and is saying that they've been committed by an asuwang, for one."

"An assoo-*what?*"

"Asuwang. It's some kind of magical creature that feeds on human hearts."

"Oh-kay..."

"We've offered our help, and so has Tory, but Sheriff Napier hasn't taken us up on it. We've also met with a coven of witches."

Silence on the other end of the call.

"Joey?"

"I'm here. Witches."

"Yeah. Rumor has it that the old woman – Margo Sardis – opened a door to Hell and left it unguarded for at least an hour. Magic apparently is commonplace here."

"Jim, I have you on speaker. Nicholas Turner is here, and has nodded his head at all of it. Apparently, such things exist." Mumbled conversation could be heard. "Okay, Nicholas says that, given that we all just came back from Hell, it's all likely to be true."

Jim laughed. "Listen, old friend, I didn't say it wasn't true. I said that it's more than we were expecting. Do we really want to continue with our presence here? I mean, I'm afraid that all of this will explode in our faces."

"Nicholas is nodding, and I agree with him. I'll ask around the other partners, but the answer is probably 'yes'. I mean, it's out of the way, and not someplace that's likely to be expected to house us. How's it coming, anyway?"

Jim began explaining the progress on the building, and the real estate dealings that had happened.

"Oh, and Brandon decided to stay with Patty for now. He's not sure that he wants to buy a place here. He says that he's afraid something will happen in

Carson City, and that he'll have to bail quickly. Selling a property doesn't allow for that."

"Understood, Jim. I'm just glad that he's there. Oh, and I'm not sure how helpful Dexter is going to be in helping Snickers with the I.T. setup. Since I have both you and Nicholas within earshot, can Snickers set everything up on his own? Would that be doable?"

Jim could hear distant conversation. "In all seriousness, I think Snickers can work wonders with any computer equipment. I say that we give him free reign."

Joey laughed. "That's basically what Nicky said. Okay, done deal. We'll be bringing him with us in a couple of days."

"PAM?"

"Yes, Mary?"

Mary turned to look at her sister. "That was *awesome!* What else can you do?"

Phoebe was still staring at the coffee mug.

"Mom? Are you okay?"

"How?" asked Phoebe tonelessly.

Pam shrugged. "I dunno, Mom. I guess that when I joined with the little ones, it jarred something loose or something. I just felt like I could do it, and I did it."

Katie looked puzzled, and said to Margo, "Aunt Margo, what the heck is going on? How did Pam get powers?"

Margo kept her face blank. "I think they've always been there. The joining just triggered them." She looked significantly at Katie.

Katie understood the look, and changed the subject. "Carol Grace, will you please take Mary and Pam outside?"

"Sure, Mom! C'mon, guys!"

The girls went outside.

Once the front door closed and the screen door slammed, Margo said, "Phoebe, can we help you with this?"

Katie sat beside her friend, and took her hand. "Phoebe, we're with you, no matter what. It's not the end of the world, you know."

Phoebe was quiet for a few seconds. Then, again in that toneless voice, she said, "What bothers me is not knowing who the father is. What kind of hideous creature would rape me twice? What possesses the magic that sired my girls, Katie?"

"Excuse me," came a voice from behind them. "That would be me. But it wasn't rape. Phoebe was an...enthusiastic participant."

"SO AN ASUWANG IS KILLING people, and I can't find a trace of it."

Kenny Pirtle sounded frustrated.

"What kind of hideous creature *is* this?" finished Pirtle.

"That's what we're trying to find out, Kenny," said Billy.

Kenny turned to Alan. "And you say that there were similar deaths in the city?"

"Yep."

"I want the M.E.'s name...I'll want to see files from his examination."

"I'll make it happen. If I can't, I'll make Tory Masterson do it."

Kenny leaned back in his chair. "And that's something else. Justice Security here in Sardis County, along with an FBI man."

"That has to stay secret, Kenny," said Billy.

"Yeah, I know. But why here? What's so special about Sardis County?"

Alan shrugged. "As far as the outside world can see, Sardis County is the armpit of the universe. Nothing happens here."

"Yeah, nothing except magic. And asuwangs. And hellhounds." Kenny noticed the look of surprise on the two lawmen's faces. "Yes, I know about the hellhound, and the open door to Hell. Lots of people in town know about it...it isn't the big secret to everyone that you hoped it would be, Billy. This county knows how to guard secrets, believe me. Justice Security is safe here. Even if the whole county knew about them, I don't think that anyone would let the cat out of the bag in fear of their own secrets being told." He stood up. "And there are a *lot* more secrets in this county that not everyone knows about." He stretched.

"But, I believe many of them will make themselves known soon, whether we want to know them or not. This place has been known for magic long before now." He walked to the door. "Get me those files, Alan. I'll see if I can find something those city folks missed. See you two later." The medical examiner left the Sheriff's office.

A minute after the door closed, Alan said, "Well. *That* was enlightening."

THE THREE WOMEN WHIRLED around to face the intruder.

Margo and Katie each had balls of blue power on their hands, ready to hurl at the first sign of danger. Phoebe stood with her eyes wide open, trying to spark some sort of remembrance of this man facing them.

The man himself was around five-ten. He had brown hair, and the bluest eyes any of the three had ever seen. He wore faded jeans, a black T-Shirt that sported the saying, "Horn Players just blow it off", sneakers, and a black derby. Hanging from the belt of his jeans was a shiny gold trumpet. A neatly trimmed beard adorned his face. He was smiling.

Katie said, with menace in her tone, "Who the hell are you? How did you get in here?"

The man chuckled. "I'll answer all of your questions, but, first, I have to take care of Phoebe's memory." He snapped his fingers as he looked into Phoebe's eyes.

It was as if a light had gone off inside Phoebe's head. She broke into a broad grin at the sight of the man standing in the living room of Junior's Farm.

"*Gabe!*" Phoebe ran to the man and hugged him fiercely.

"Hey, whoa, wait a minute, Phoebe! You're a married woman now!" The man laughed as he peeled Phoebe's arms from around his neck. He held her at arm's length and looked into her eyes. "Phoebe, I'm sorry that I had to close off the memories of our time together. It was safer for the children that way."

Margo let the blue power ball fade. "Katie, I think it's all right. You can let the power go."

Katie's brow furrowed. "Are you sure, Aunt Margo?"

Margo nodded.

Katie let the power ball fade. "I'm keeping it handy anyway. Just in case."

"Gabe, what's going on? Where have you been?" asked Phoebe.

"Would it be too much trouble to tell you over a cup of coffee? I haven't had a good cup of coffee for such a long time!"

Katie relented. "Sure. Let's go to the kitchen. We can sit at the table."

THE FIRST TRUCK THAT Patty wanted to open was the one that carried Flame.

The longhorn came down the ramp and into the pasture. She saw Patty, and immediately began lowing as she hurried over to her owner.

Patty began laughing as she hugged the old steer's neck. "Hi, old girl! I sure did miss you!"

If cows could smile, Flame was grinning ear-to-ear.

Brandon was smiling, too, happy that his friend was reunited with her pet.

Patty moved around in front of Flame. She held up a halter so that Flame could see it. "Flame, want me to show you the pond? We can ride down there."

Brandon nudged two of the truck drivers. "Watch this, guys. I bet you've never seen anything like this."

The drivers turned to watch as Patty easily slipped the halter around Flame's head, fastening it over the steer's horns. Once it was secured, Patty climbed up onto Flame's back.

"Come on, girl! I know you're thirsty!"

Patty rode the longhorn across the pasture to the pond that was located behind the barn. Many of the other steers followed closely behind, while others grazed.

"I'll be damned," said Joe Mills.

Brandon laughed. "Those cattle saved Patty's ass in Carson City. They love her!" He chuckled again. "Don't tell her that I told you this, but people in Carson City started calling her 'Cow Patty' because of it! We're thinking of changing the name of the casino to 'Cow Patty's'. Patty isn't convinced that it's a better name than 'Big Daddy's', and she sure as hell doesn't like 'Cow Patty', so it may not happen."

"ALAN, WHO DO YOU THINK the asuwang is masquerading as?" asked Billy.

"No idea, Billy. It could be anyone."

"What about those cases in the city? What did the police learn?"

Alan looked speculative. "Well, initial reports said that a young woman was seen at each of the nightclubs. She was there at the same time as the victims, and was seen dancing with every single one of them. Reports said that she was extremely beautiful. One of the detectives that staked out the clubs even labeled her 'Hot Child'. The name stuck."

"And the murders stopped?"

"They did, right after Detective Coleman died. It looks like he was the last victim."

"But, if an asuwang can alter its appearance, and if it's the same one, it might not necessarily be camouflaged as female. It could be hiding behind a male mask, too. Right?"

"Possibly."

Billy looked at his friend. "You know that I hate this shit, right?"

Alan smiled. "Yep."

"Let's go grab some lunch. Want to eat with our ladies?"

Alan stood. "Sure! Let's head to the farm."

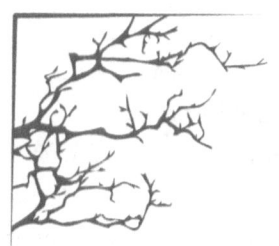

Chapter 8

Phoebe and Margo sat at the kitchen table with Gabe, as Katie made a second pot of coffee. Pam's cup had finished off the first pot.

"You said that it was safer for the children if I didn't remember our time together. Why?" Phoebe's question was full of pain.

Margo eyed the man closely.

"Phoebe...have Pam and Mary shown any magical inclinations?"

"Yes. Especially when they hold hands with Carol Grace."

"Carol Grace is Katie's daughter? Descendant of the Sardis witches?"

Phoebe nodded.

"Good. Things are happening the way they should."

Margo's head perked up at the comment. "What do you mean, 'the way they should'?"

"I was wondering that myself," added Katie.

Gabe took a breath, and waved his hands around as he spoke. "All of this...Sardis County...has suddenly become a battleground. It will remain that way for some time."

"A battleground? What kind of battleground?"

"A battleground between the forces of Heaven and Hell." He turned to look at Phoebe. "And you do remember that all four of your children are ours, don't you?"

Phoebe nodded. "Yes."

Margo and Katie looked stunned.

Katie spoke first. "Derek? *And* Catherine?"

Phoebe nodded shyly.

"But you were married to the methhead then!"

"No, she wasn't," said Gabe. "Phoebe's never been married until now. It was a false memory that I planted in both of their minds. It was for Phoebe's safety...and the children's."

"You mean that they might start showing magic, too?" asked Margo.

"Any time now," answered Gabe. "And the magic grows with each child."

"And I also remember that I'm *not* an alcoholic," declared Phoebe.

Gabe nodded. "Another false memory. Across the whole county, as a matter of fact. I can fix that." He snapped his fingers.

Katie suddenly had memories of Phoebe as a laughing, happy young woman. She sat back abruptly in her chair. "Oh, my God! Phoebe, I remember!" She looked at Gabe. "And I remember seeing *you* around town back then!"

Margo said with annoyance, "I don't remember anything." She leaned forward, looking Gabe directly in the eyes. "I want to know who you are, Mister. Right now."

Gabe looked puzzled. "You mean you haven't guessed?"

Margo looked the man over. The resemblance to Chuck Mangione aside, she worked it all over in her mind. *Trumpet hanging at his side. Magic that happens with a snap of his fingers. Magical children, and the ability to alter memories. And his name is...*

"Gabriel!" she said with wonder.

Gabe nodded. "I am."

"Wait a minute," said Katie. "Gabriel? *The* Gabriel?"

Gabe smiled. "One and the same."

Katie pointed to the trumpet. "And is that...?"

Gabe nodded. "I've never played this one. I'm only allowed to play it once, and that order comes from...well, you know. When He is tired of His creation, He'll order me to play it...and I will."

"So, you're the source of Mary's magic," speculated Margo. "And Pam's."

"Only half of their power," answered Gabe. He pointed at Phoebe. "*She* supplied the other half."

Phoebe wore a demure look.

Katie said, "Phoebe? How?"

Gabe smiled at Katie's perplexed look. "She's your cousin. One of the Sardis men played around on the other side of the sheets...I won't name him, either. He's doing his penance in the afterlife. But, Phoebe is descended from him. Phoebe is as much a Sardis witch as you are."

KENNY PIRTLE WAS EXAMINING some of the killer's non-evidence in his lab.

The Medical Examiner's office was located in the building next door to the Sheriff's office. The lab was in the back of the building, and so was the morgue. Kenny was inside the lab.

Everyone had gone to lunch. All of the staff had tried to talk Kenny into going with them over to Ethel's Diner, but he had begged off.

Kenny was alone in the building.

He was so engrossed in the reports from his medical techs, the FBI lab, and law enforcement, that he didn't hear anyone come into the lab.

"Hello, Kenny."

Kenny jumped. He whirled around and saw who had spoken. "Oh! You scared me!"

"Good."

"I can't find a damn thing in these...what? *Good?*"

The visitor nodded.

"Why good?"

The visitor smiled. The smile widened as the visitor's face elongated. "Because I'm your boogie man."

Kenny's eyes widened in surprise, and the asuwang began to feed once more.

ALAN LED THE WAY UP the porch steps, with Billy close behind.

Pam, Mary, and Carol Grace had just walked back from the mailbox, and followed the men onto the porch.

"Hi, girls," said Alan. "Pam, I hope you slept well. How do you feel?"

"Great, sir," answered Pam.

Carol Grace gave Alan a huge hug. Mary hugged Billy.

"Ask Pam what she did today," said Carol Grace.

"Yeah, you just won't believe it," added Mary.

"How about we grab some lunch first?" said Alan.

"Yeah, my stomach sounds like a bear has taken up residence," said Billy.

The girls agreed, and walked into the house giggling. Alan and Billy followed.

"Hi, Katie! I hope there's some lunch ready, because you have five hungry people..." Alan stopped talking as the group walked into the kitchen.

Gabe smiled and stood. "Hello, Deputy Blake." He held out his hand to Alan. "I've been enjoying your hospitality, and I'm very grateful."

Puzzled, Alan said, "My pleasure. And you are...?"

"Oh, I'm sorry. Call me Gabe." Gabe turned to Billy. "Hello, Sheriff Napier." He held out his hand to Billy. "You and I have some things to discuss. But, first, let me take care of you and Alan's memories." He snapped his fingers.

Both men's eyes widened as the memories rushed into their heads.

Billy immediately looked at Phoebe, with a question in his eyes. "He's back?"

Phoebe went to Billy. "He's from the past, Billy. You're my life and my future." Into his ear, she whispered, "Gabe is only the children's father. That's all."

Billy searched his wife's eyes and saw the truth there. He nodded to her, and smiled. Inside, he felt relief.

Alan said, "Okay, I vaguely remember you, Gabe, from right around our senior year, but that's all. What's going on? Who are you?"

Gabe had noticed the children. His eyes widened. After a moment, he walked over to them. To Carol Grace, he said, "Could you excuse me, please? I need to talk to Pam and Mary."

Carol Grace, who hadn't seen this man come into the farmhouse, looked at her mother.

Katie nodded.

Carol Grace stepped aside.

Katie saw that Carol Grace was casting a spell under her breath. From the way her daughter held her right hand, it was the same fireball spell that Katie had kept ready.

Gabe looked from Pam to Mary. He had tears in his eyes.

Pam cocked her head slightly. "You look familiar. Who are you, sir?"

Wiping away tears, Gabe said, "I'm sorry. Here." He snapped his fingers.

A look of glee came to Pam's face. *"Daddy!"* She threw herself into Gabe's arms.

"Hi, baby, you're all grown up now!"

"Pam, who is this guy?" asked Mary.

"Oh, Mary, you were probably too young to remember him! This is our father, Gabriel."

Mary crossed her arms and eyed Gabe. "If you're my father, why haven't you been around?"

Gabe looked ashamed. "I'm sorry, Mary. But I've kept an eye on you ever since you were born. I've been following His orders, and now I have some time to spend with you."

"Whose orders?" asked Mary bluntly.

Gabe looked directly into Mary's eyes. "The one in charge of the realm that is called 'Heaven'. I'm what you call an 'angel', and you, your sisters, and your brother are all my children. You are Nephilim."

Billy's jaw dropped open with realization. "Gabriel?" He looked down at the trumpet attached to Gabe's waist by a length of chain. "You aren't going to blow that, are you?"

Gabe laughed. "No."

Alan said, "So, you're the reason that Pam and Mary have magic?"

"Partially. Their mother contributed her half, too."

"Huh?" said Billy. "'Her half'? What are you saying, Gabe?"

"Maybe you guys should all sit down," said Phoebe. "We've got news to share."

FLAME NUZZLED BRANDON as he looked up at Patty.

Brandon laughed. "Stop, Flame! That tickles!" To Patty, he said, "What are you going to do for food for them?"

Patty, still sitting on Flame's broad back, said, "I've got pasture land, and I'm going into town later. I'll hit up the feed store, and see if I can buy some hay and some corn for treats. I'll also ask them for a veterinarian recommendation. I have to shop for furniture, too. Wanna come with?"

"Sure. Does Jim need us at all today?"

Patty smiled. "I guess not. He hasn't called us, and I didn't even think to call him. We can stop by his house when we go into town. We haven't seen it yet, anyway."

"Sure!"

MARY MASTERSON WALKED with her husband and toddler son. They were walking through downtown Perry.

"Tory, I love this town," said Mary. "I feel good about raising Adam here."

Tory had kept the stories about the murders as far away from his wife as possible. He also hadn't mentioned that magic was prominent in the county, either. He was carrying a small Beretta semi-automatic under the tail of his polo shirt. Asuwangs, witches, creatures of Hell...he'd shoot any of them that came close to his wife or son. The only reason that he hadn't reported any of it to the Bureau was that he figured they'd think he had lost his mind. "I'm so glad that you do, honey."

"And the deal on the house was fantastic!"

Tory kept watching everything. Well-trained, he missed nothing. "Uh-huh."

Mary noticed that Tory was distracted. She smiled to herself. Time to bring her husband back to reality. "We're having the Sardis Slasher over for dinner on Tuesday. And Margo Sardis is training me as a witch."

"That's great, honey...wait, *what?*"

Mary laughed. Adam, even though he didn't understand what his mother was laughing at, nevertheless laughed right along with her.

"Tory, you have to stop worrying about me, and you *really* have to stop trying to shield me from things. You used to do that to me when we lived in Chicago, and you're *still* doing it!" Mary waved her hand, indicating the town. "This is Small Town America, darling. Hard to keep secrets, especially at a beauty parlor, or Mackie's grocery store. I know what you're up against, and I bet you're having a hard time believing. Right?"

She knows me too well, thought Tory. *That's what happens when you fall in love with and marry your best friend. I wonder if Patty knows that?* Out loud, he said, "Yes, I am. How can magic be real?"

"How can angels be real? How can God exist? How can Hell exist? You believe in those things, don't you? Like a good little Catholic boy?"

"Of course, Mary. But it's not the same thing!"

Mary had an incredulous look on her face. "Tory Beauregard Masterson! Of *course* it's the same thing! Magic comes from..."

A scream interrupted her. The couple whirled to see a woman standing outside the Medical Examiner's office. As they noticed her, the woman screamed again.

Tory took his wife's arm. "Mary! Take Adam and go to Ethel's Diner! Now! Stay there until you hear from me!"

Mary nodded, and picked up Adam. As she moved in the diner's direction, Tory drew his Beretta and FBI credentials, and ran to the screaming woman. He barely beat a couple of uniformed deputies. He flashed his credentials at the deputies. They nodded their understanding.

"Tory Masterson, FBI! What's wrong, ma'am?"

The woman pointed to the building behind her. "In there! It's Kenny Pirtle! He's...oh, *God!*" She screamed again.

Tory pointed to one of the deputies. "You take care of her! Take her to the Sheriff's office!" He pointed to the second deputy. "You come with me!"

The deputy followed Tory into the building. Both men had their guns drawn, and looked into each room as they made their way down the hall. When they reached the lab's door, they both entered with guns drawn.

Kenny Pirtle was lying on a lab table. His body was strapped to the table by the wrists, ankles, and upper torso. His skin was pale, and his chest cavity had been sliced open and peeled back. The ribs had been broken off, apparently to provide easy access to the heart. It looked as if all of Pirtle's organs were stacked on the big scales. On the wall above Pirtle's head were the words, "I'm your Boogie Man". It looked as if the words had been written with the Medical Examiner's blood. No blood had been spilled anywhere that Tory could see.

"Oh, boy," said Tory under his breath.

Both lawmen backed out of the lab.

Outside the doors, Tory said, "You guard the door. I'll call Sheriff Napier. Don't let anyone in."

The deputy nodded his understanding.

Tory holstered his gun and took out his phone. He had programmed the Sheriff's number into his phone.

"Napier."

"This is Tory Masterson. You have another murder."

"Damn! Will you call the Medical Examiner? I'll need him."

"Pirtle's already at the scene, Sheriff. He's the victim."

WHEN BILLY AND ALAN had sat down at the table, Pam and the two younger children sat down on the floor. Little Bit climbed into Carol Grace's lap.

Gabe explained everything about the Sardis connection.

Mary looked at Carol Grace. "We're *cousins*? Yay!"

The two girls gave each other a high five.

"I'm married to a Sardis witch?" asked a stunned Billy.

Phoebe smiled as she wrapped her arms around him. "You sure are, big boy."

Alan punched Billy lightly on the arm. "Hey, I have no complaints at all. Being married to Katie is the best thing that ever happened to me! And I'm so very in love with her, too." He gazed at Katie.

Katie looked back at Alan and smiled.

Gabe looked at Pam and Mary. His love for them was obvious to everyone. "And you two are also half-angels, born of an angel and a human...or, in this case, a witch. Your powers are astronomical. Only part of them have appeared so far, but more will make their appearances as time goes on." Gabe leaned against the kitchen counter. "I think the deep friendship between Mary and Carol Grace, and the connection and magical powers when they joined hands, is from the Sardis side. Pam's joining amplified the effect. But, your angelic powers haven't appeared as of yet. When they do, nothing evil will be able to stand."

Billy's phone rang. It was Tory. When Billy disconnected the call, he looked blankly at Alan. "That was Masterson. Kenny Pirtle is dead. The asuwang fed again."

Alan stood. "Let's go."

Billy, looking defeated, glanced around at the people in the room. "If any of you has any way of detecting the asuwang, I'd appreciate it. I need all the help I can get."

Gabe looked pained. "I'm sorry, Billy, but I can't help you. I have orders."

Billy nodded. "Understood."

Katie hooked her arm through Alan's. She looked at Billy. "Aunt Margo and I will keep trying, Billy. We'll come up with something."

"And now that we know that Phoebe is a Sardis, we'll throw that into it, too," added Margo. "You go on and do what you have to, Billy."

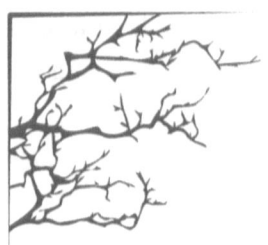

Chapter 9

Emily Owen answered the knock at Jim Dandy's front door.

Patty Ferguson's eyes watched as Brandon King's eyes widened in surprise.

Emily smiled at the two.

"Hi, Patty! Hello, Brandon!"

"Emily!" Brandon shouted. Both young people hugged the woman.

"Emily, is that those two rich kids?" said a voice from the study.

"Yes, it is," called Emily, with a big smile still plastered onto her face.

"Well, bring them inside! Don't leave them on the front porch! What will the neighbors say?"

All three of them laughed as Brandon and Patty entered Jim's home.

Emily led the way to the study. Jim stood as they entered.

"Welcome, guys!" Jim held out his hand to Brandon. Brandon took it, and they shook. "What do you think of the house so far?"

Patty said, "It looks great, Jim!"

Jim nodded. "And it was one hell of a bargain, too!"

Patty looked puzzled. "Hmm. My farm was a bargain, too. Do you think..."

Jim's phone rang. He looked at it, and said, "Hey, it's Tory. Hold on, guys. Emily, show them the house, would you?" He answered his phone. "Tory! How's the FBI man settling in on this fine day?"

Emily said, "Come on, let me show you the kitchen. It's to die for!"

Just as the trio stepped out of the study and into the hall, Jim called out. "Hey, guys! Tory called a red alert! There's been another murder! This time, it was the medical examiner!"

"GABE?"

"Yes, Miss Margo?"

"Why are you here? I mean, why now?"

Pam, Phoebe, Katie, and Margo all sat at the kitchen table with Gabriel. Carol Grace and Mary had gone upstairs to practice on some spells that Margo had assigned, and to do some homework. Little Bit appeared from under the recliner in the living room, and followed the girls upstairs.

Gabe squirmed in his seat. "Well...mainly, it's...um..."

Phoebe laughed. "Come on, Gabe, spit it out!"

Gabe looked determined. "It's because of you, Miss Margo. It's because of what you did, and because of what an angel did."

Margo leaned heavily back in her chair. Katie looked shocked. Pam looked from her father to her mother, and then to Katie and Margo.

"What I did?" asked Margo. "What do you mean, Gabe?" *Although I can probably guess,* thought Margo.

Gabe had a troubled look on his face. "Okay, here goes...according to the big guy, you opened a portal to Hell, right?"

Margo nodded slowly. *I thought so.* "I did. And I regret doing it far more than you know."

Gabe nodded agreement. "He knows you regret it, and He forgives you. The trouble is, the portal allowed a huge number of the residents of Hell to come through to this plane of existence." He looked around the table at the four women. "Opening the portal and allowing the demons to come through wasn't the big deal. Sending them back isn't the problem, although it will take some time. Opening the portal wasn't really the problem, because portals between the realms open more often than most know, but no one knows where or when. The problem comes when you combine the opening of the portal and the fact that an angel was caught entering Hell."

"Why is that a big deal, Daddy?" asked Pam.

Gabriel smiled at his daughter. "If an angel enters Hell, or if a demon enters Heaven, it's considered an act of war."

Four sets of eyes widened.

"Are you saying that an angel entered Hell?" asked Katie.

Gabe nodded.

"Then are we at war with Hell?"

"Katie, we're doing everything that we can to avoid it. I'm here just in case."

"Just in case?" asked Phoebe.

Gabe shrugged. "My Father is going to win...no matter what," he said with simplicity.

"Will you tell us about the angel?" asked Pam.

The angel nodded. "I'll tell you what I'm allowed to tell. This is confidential, and can't be shared with husbands, boyfriends, or the younger children. Agreed?"

The ladies all nodded acquiescence.

"Okay. Eleven years ago, one of us chose to be born into a human being. We do that occasionally, to remind us of how connected we are to our Father's creations. But, the woman that carried the child developed a fast form of uterine cancer, and died. The child also died before it was ever born." He paused, then said to Katie, "May I have a cup of coffee, Katie? It's one of the things that I love about this place."

Katie smiled. "Of course." She rose to get it.

Pam stopped her. "Let me, Katie, please?"

Katie nodded.

Pam closed her eyes and reached her hand out. A cup floated down from the cupboard, and gently settled on the kitchen counter next to the coffee pot. The pot of coffee gently extracted itself from the heat plate, poured some of its contents into the cup, and placed itself back in its housing. The cup rose from the counter, and floated to the table. It set itself down in front of Gabriel. Once the cup was in place, Pam opened her eyes and smiled at her father.

Gabriel beamed at Pam. "Great job, Pam! I'm very proud of you!"

Pam blushed and looked down. "Thank you, Daddy."

Gabe took a sip from the cup and continued. "So, this angel made a choice. She decided to stay with the unborn child and her mother, in Heaven, and to grow as a normal human child." He looked at Pam. "See, she's half-angel, too, just like you." He drank coffee. "Except for one little thing."

"What's that, Daddy?"

"When an angel chooses to be reborn into a human for that span of life, the angel's memory is wiped. It has no recollection of being an angel." He drank coffee. "Man, that's good! Thank you, Katie." He placed the cup on the table. "Because she chose to remain in Heaven with her mother, this angel has her full memory. She now has chosen to spend time with her human father on earth. She has full human DNA, and full angelic powers. She is a force to be reckoned with."

"What drove this angel to enter Hell?" asked Phoebe. "It sounds like a foolish thing to do."

Gabe closed his eyes, and he seemed that he hadn't heard.

"Gabe?"

Gabe held up one finger. "Hold on, I'm asking how much I can tell you. If I tell you too much, it could alter the path of things."

After a moment, he opened his eyes.

"I can tell you four all of it, as long as it's understood that *Carol Grace and Mary can't know any of it.* They are critical to this angel's path, but. *They. Can't. Know.*" With each word, he looked from Margo to Katie to Phoebe. Once the final word was spoken, his gaze rested on Pam. "The Father says you can speak of it among the four of you, but not to those two...or anyone else. That means husbands, boyfriends, or people you might have met that were part of it. Do each of you understand...and agree?"

The four women nodded solemnly.

"Okay. The angel's name on this plane is Madeline Turner. She's the daughter of Nicholas Turner, of Justice Security."

Katie and Phoebe's mouths gaped open in surprise.

Gabe half-smiled, and continued. "Thirty-seven children, along with their bus driver, were kidnapped recently..."

Katie spoke up. "We saw that on the news! The kidnappers wanted Joey Justice in exchange for the children's freedom, didn't they? And their location was booby-trapped...I think to explode by a certain time if their demands weren't met. Weren't the kidnappers killed in an explosion?"

Gabe nodded. "Yes. And they were sent to Hell as penance. But they were killed before they could disclose the location of the children. Marcus Moore, the head honcho of the FBI in the city, had called in Nicholas Turner and Madeline earlier that day to consult on the case. Justice Security offered Nicholas a partnership, and he accepted. Fast forward to the point that the kidnappers were killed. Justice Security had no way to find out the location of the children before the deadline."

Gabe stood, and went to the coffee pot once more. As he filled his cup, he said, "So, Joey got this grand idea..."

Pam blurted. "I bet he wanted Madeline to go to Hell and look for the kidnappers."

Gabe turned and smiled. "Good guess, daughter! But, he didn't just want Madeline to go. He wanted them *all* to go. He and Nicholas would look for the head kidnapper, while the others would help Madeline if they were discovered."

Gabe leaned against the kitchen counter, and sipped coffee. "If you haven't guessed, they were discovered, all right. Dexter Beck's wife, Megan, was captured and taken away by demons, and Madeline was almost killed by a bolt of black energy. They all would have died if not for the intervention of another angel...Michael. He was able to save Madeline's life, but he couldn't restore her memory of how to be an angel. She knows that she's half human, full angel, but she can't remember how to do it." He sipped again. "That's where Mary and Carol Grace come into the picture. Nicholas Turner is moving here with his family, to Sardis County. Somehow, and I haven't been told how, Mary and Carol Grace will help Madeline restore her memories and her full power."

Gabe smiled at the women. "And may Father help whatever Hellspawn tries to tangle with *that* triangle of power!"

Upstairs, the group heard a door slam. They could hear Carol Grace and Mary talking and coming down the stairs, and Little Bit barked excitedly as she followed the girls. They careened into the kitchen.

"Mom, we're going outside!" called Carol Grace.

"Is that okay?" asked Mary.

Both women looked to Gabriel, who smiled and nodded. Both women smiled at the girls.

"Sure. Be back inside in an hour, please," answered Phoebe.

"We have dinner to make, and I have a feeling we'll have lots of folks to feed. We'll need help from you two," added Katie.

"Okay, Mom!" called Carol Grace.

The two girls and the dog slammed out the back door.

Margo shook her head, with a half-smile. "Oh, to be that young again, and with all that energy!"

Gabe smiled. "Miss Margo, I hope you can keep some energy. If this war breaks out, we'll need your power."

BILLY LOOKED AROUND the coroner's office, hoping to find something to lead him to the killer. Alan was questioning the woman that found Pirtle.

Tory stood beside Billy, also looking for some sort of clue.

Teddy Baker was taking photos of the crime scene.

Tory happened to be looking at Baker as the photographer moved the camera away from his face. He saw something that puzzled him.

The photographer had a half-smile on his face.

Before Tory could ask the man what was so humorous about another murder, Jim Dandy called to him from the lab door.

With reluctance, Tory turned from his curiosity and faced his friend.

"What happened, Tory?" asked Jim.

Tory shook his head. "Not sure, Jim. I was walking around town with Mary and Adam when I heard that lady scream." Tory gestured to the woman. "I arrived on the scene at the same time as two deputies. We searched the place, and found Pirtle as you see him."

Jim looked around the lab. "Think it would help if I had Patty and Brandon canvas around downtown?"

Tory took a breath. "That would be great, but I would really appreciate if someone could go to Ethel's and retrieve Mary and Adam. I'd feel better if someone escorted them home and mad sure that they're safe."

Jim nodded. "Emily's here, too. I'll send her right away."

"Thank you, Jim. I appreciate it."

"Hey! Tory!" called Billy. "Can you come here a moment?"

"Sure." Tory made his way over to the Sheriff.

Billy looked at the FBI man. "Tory, I'm in a damned bad spot. Would the Bureau be willing to send in a complete forensic team, including a person that can perform medical examiner duties? I've got to have some help here, or I'm screwed."

"I don't see why not. I'll get on the phone to Marcus right away." Tory had forgotten the thing that had puzzled him.

CAROL GRACE, MARY, and Little Bit had walked to the barn. A bale of straw rested outside the big doors, and the girls sat down. They took turns throwing a small, Little Bit-sized tennis ball, entertaining the puppy as they chatted.

"So, now you know who your father is," said Carol Grace. She glanced at Mary. "That makes you half-angel."

"I know."

"Maybe that's where the stuff comes from when we hold hands."

Little Bit brought the ball to Mary, and dropped it into her hand. She sat back, panting happily. Mary picked up the ball and threw it. Little Bit scrambled after it. Watching the puppy chase the bouncing ball, Mary answered. "Maybe so, Carol Grace, but..."

Carol Grace glanced at her friend. "But what?"

Mary looked down at the ground. "I'm scared."

Carol Grace watched her friend for a few seconds. Then, she put her arm around Mary's shoulders. The girls put their heads together. "So am I, Mary."

Little Bit had spotted a squirrel beside the barn, and happily chased it.

"That spell we cast so that we could listen to the adults' conversation?" said Mary. "I don't want to do that again, Carol Grace. There are some things we don't need to know."

"But now we know that we're supposed to help another angel. I like that."

"Yeah, that's good. But this talk about a war with Hell? I *don't* like that."

"But your dad said that it might not happen...that it's only a possibility."

Mary looked at her friend. "We could ask."

Carol Grace looked puzzled. "Ask who? Your dad?"

"No. We could...join hands. Ask our own questions."

Carol Grace glanced at the house. "We'll have to go behind the barn."

EMILY OWENS CALLED her boyfriend, Turk Wendell, as she walked to Ethel's Diner.

"Justice Security. This is Tony Armstrong. How may I direct your call?"

"Hi, Tony! This is Emily. Would you transfer me to Turk?"

Emily could hear the smile in Tony's voice as he answered. "Of course I will! Maybe he'll say more than five words to you at once."

Emily laughed as she heard the click from being placed on hold. After a few seconds, she heard the voice of the man she was falling in love with.

"Justice Security. This is Turk."

"I only have a minute, big man. There's been another death here."

"Hey, baby. Who died this time?"

"Medical examiner. Pirtle."

"Aw, hell! You safe, Em?"

Emily smiled. "I'm fine, Turk. Don't say anything, okay? I think Jim wants to tell Joey about it."

"Will do, baby. Gonna see you soon?"

"As soon as I can. You can come here, too, you know."

"Hmpf. Might get my heart ate. It's awful big."

Emily laughed. "Gotta go, big man."

"Okay. 'Bye."

Emily tucked her cell phone into her back pocket and walked into Ethel's. She looked around and spotted Mary Masterson sitting in a booth. Adam Masterson was happily seated in a high chair at the end of the table. Mary looked up at Emily and waved. Emily waved back and walked over to the FBI man's wife and son.

"Let me guess," said Mary. "Tory sent you to make sure that we get home safely."

Emily smiled. "You guessed it."

Mary smiled back. "Tory has always been very protective of me. I'm glad that he cares so much, but he *can* be overprotective."

Adam smiled a toothless smile at his mother.

"Please sit, Emily, and tell me about this one."

Emily sat, facing the door of the deserted diner. "Same M.O. as the others. No blood, but no clues. Internal organs arranged in some kind of pattern. No heart."

Mary nodded. "And I heard that it was the M.E.?"

"Yes."

Mary spooned some eggs from a jar into Adam's mouth. "Are you worried, Emily?"

Emily thought for a moment. "Yes. I am." She shifted her gaze to Adam, and the baby goggled at her, then smiled toothlessly. "Jim said that the killer was called an asuwang. I don't know what that is, but I understand that it can shape-shift. How do you fight something like that?"

Mary took a sip of her coffee. "What do you think about all the talk about witches and magic and all of that other stuff?"

"Oh, I believe it all!" No hesitation.

Mary looked at Emily. "Really?"

"You didn't meet Madeline, did you?"

"No."

"Neither did I, but I heard all about her. An honest-to-gosh half-angel! And part of Justice Security!" Emily crossed herself. "I'm a good Catholic, Mary, and I believe that angels walk among us all the time. So, how can I be a good Catholic and *not* believe in all of that?"

Ethel brought over a coffee pot and refilled Mary's cup. "Need anything else, hon?"

"No, thank you, Ethel. Little man here is almost done."

Ethel turned to Emily. "How about you, sweetie? Can I bring you anything?"

Emily smiled at the woman. "No, thank you, Ethel."

Ethel turned to leave, but Emily stopped her with a question.

"Ethel?"

"Yes, sweetie?"

"Do you know Margo Sardis?"

"I should say so! More years than I care to count!"

"Is she really a witch?"

Ethel looked from Emily to Mary. "Oh, girls, without a doubt! One of the most powerful Sardis witches I've heard tell of! Some say that that niece of hers – Katie – is almost as powerful...but I can't say myself."

Emily asked, "Is she a good witch, or a bad one?"

Ethel pondered for a moment. "She's likely like all of us, sweetie. Mostly good. I would have heard otherwise." She abruptly turned and walked behind the lunch counter to replace the coffee pot.

"MARCUS, THE SHERIFF here needs the Bureau's help."

"What does he need, Tory?"

"He desperately needs forensic people. Lots of them. I'm talking lab equipment, autopsy capabilities, and someone to act as medical examiner. The Sardis County M.E. just became the latest murder victim."

"Done. Does he need law enforcement or investigative help?"

"No, Marcus, he didn't ask for that. He has reliable deputies, myself, and the Justice Security personnel that are already here. It's things on the forensic side that he's lacking. He's frustrated because there hasn't been a single trace of evidence. No hair, no particles, no prints."

"The team I'm sending should be able to find something. I'll chopper them out to you. They should be there soon. Portable lab facilities will take six to seven hours, though...they'll have to drive."

"Understood, sir. Thank you."

"Hey, gotta keep the locals cooperative. It might help keep our secret." Marcus didn't speak for a couple of beats. "Tory, Nicholas says that your killer is some sort of creature."

"That's what we've been told."

"You don't believe it?"

Tory paused. "Jury's still out."

Marcus lost his jovial tone. He spoke with seriousness. "Tory, believe it. Don't doubt it. I'm living proof in believing, and I believe it with all my heart, both personal and professional. This thing is a *thing*, and it's damned dangerous. Take no chances. Am I clear?"

Tory was somewhat taken aback. The FBI chief had never spoke to him with such conviction. "Y-yes, sir."

"You're a good agent, Tory, and a good liaison for Justice Security. Learn to take things at face value, and proceed as if what you've been told is real.

It usually is." Tory could hear Marcus turning pages. "One more thing, though...make sure that nobody says the words 'magic', 'asuwang', or anything else not grounded in the world. We don't need those things getting out, and we don't want to be laughing stocks. Understood?"

"Yes, sir."

"Okay, kid, I gotta go. I got medical people to get to you."

"Thanks, Marcus. For everything."

"No problem, Tory. I'll have the chopper contact you through your cell phone once they're almost there. You can give them a good place to park."

Tory hung up, tucked his phone back into his pocket, and went to find the sheriff.

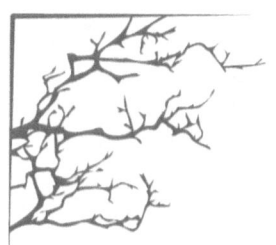

Chapter 10

"**A**unt Margo, would you please go find the girls?" asked Katie. "I want them to set the table, and they haven't come back inside."

Margo rose from the table. "Sure, Katie. I bet they lost track of time."

Katie grinned. "I bet they're gossiping somewhere." She glanced at Gabriel. "Or Mary could be talking about things that she has to adjust to."

Margo nodded. "Back in a jiffy."

The old woman went out the kitchen door to the screened-in back porch. She crossed it, opened the screen door, and went down the steps to the back yard.

This stuff is worse than anything I ever thought could happen. We're fighting some kind of creature, Gabriel has returned and told us about a possible war with Hell, and the girls are supposed to bring back an angel's memory. Margo smiled to herself. *Living is Sardis County sure is interesting.*

Margo stopped in the middle of the back yard. She looked toward the barn.

Little Bit was half squatting, with her front paws bent down. The little pug was looking at something behind the barn, and she was whining.

Oh, crap.

Margo walked in the direction of the barn. As she walked, she readied a powerful defensive spell. The power stirred itself into a glowing white ball around her hand.

"Little Bit! Come here!" called Margo.

The dog looked back at Margo, squatted again, and barked. She looked back at whatever was behind the barn, then looked at Margo and barked again.

The girls!

Margo began moving as fast as she could toward the back of the barn. As she turned the corner, she gasped.

Hanging in the air, three feet from the ground, inside a blue protective force bubble, were Carol Grace and Mary. They were holding hands, as usual, and their eyes were rolled so far back into their sockets that only the whites were visible. No sound came from them, but their lips moved. First Carol Grace, then Mary.

Realization hit the old witch.

They're having conversations!

Mary smiled.

Carol Grace looked puzzled for a moment, and her lips moved again. Her head slowly cocked to one side a bit.

They're asking their own questions! And they're getting answers!

Although their eyes were still rolled up to whites, both girls turned their heads slowly to face Margo.

Margo felt an unreasonable chill.

Abruptly, the force bubble winked out. The girls slowly drifted down so that their feet were touching the ground again.

Now they'll pass out, and I'll have to get help to carry them inside.

But the girls merely woke up. Their eyes rolled into place, and they released each other's hands.

Carol Grace and Mary ran to the old witch.

"Aunt Margo! We know how to kill the asuwang, and *we know how to find out who it is!*" said Carol Grace.

Mary added, "And it's *pregnant!*"

BILLY WAS LOCKING DOWN the medical examiner's office. Tory had told him what the FBI was sending, and Billy didn't want to take a chance on contaminating the crime scene. It was best if no one went inside.

Alan was talking to some Perry city policemen and some deputies, explaining that Billy planned to turn the whole thing over to the FBI. He was throwing in the towel on this investigation. Alan knew that giving it to the FBI stuck in Billy's craw...hell, it stuck in his *own* craw! But, sometimes, you have to let the big boys give it a try.

"So, Billy says that we're locking it down until the FBI people arrive. They're flying in now, and will be landing shortly. We're letting them land in the parking lot behind City Hall. Portable forensic labs are coming by highway, and should be here not long after the forensic team begin work."

One city policeman asked, "What do you want us to do now, Alan?"

Alan took a breath. "Surround the building. Make sure that it stays secure. Agent Tory Masterson will meet the FBI people and escort them here. Once they're here, you"...he pointed at one deputy..."will let them into the building. Maintain security, and get those folks anything they need, even if it's just some chewing gum from the big box."

Acknowledgements came from the law enforcement gathering. Off to one side stood Jim Dandy, Emily Owens, Patty Ferguson, and Brandon King. Alan walked over to them.

Jim said, "Alan, do you want us to do anything?"

"Yeah," Alan said. "Come to my place for dinner. You've met most of the crowd, and Billy will be there. Tory, too, if he thinks he can tear away from the forensic people. Emily, would you mind gathering Tory's wife and son? I know we'd love to have them over, too."

"Home cooked?" asked Brandon.

Alan smiled. "You bet!"

Brandon nudged Patty. "Let's go, girl."

Alan's phone rang. He looked down at it and saw Katie's name. He smiled and answered.

"Hi, good-lookin'!"

"Alan, when are you coming home?"

Alan sensed her concerned tone. "Soon. What's wrong, Katie?"

Katie took a breath. "Carol Grace and Mary have some things to tell you. Bring Billy."

"Will do. I love you."

"I love you, too."

They disconnected.

"Something wrong, Alan?" asked Jim.

"Something's up with the girls. Let me go gather Billy." He waved at the group. "See you guys shortly!"

THE ASUWANG, DISGUISED in its human form, watched from the crowd gathered around the medical examiners building.

Fools. This is why they'll never be anything more than prey.

The asuwang's digestive system gurgled.

Again? Already?

THE THING STOPPED AT the fence. Something was different.

A single longhorn stood in the pasture, a bit farther down the fence line. It snorted, and lowed, sounding nervous. Its head was up, and it was watching the thing.

The thing's attention was drawn by the sound. Suddenly, a long tentacle snapped out and grabbed the longhorn. The tentacle retracted quickly, faster than the longhorn could sound an alarm.

The only sounds were small noises as the thing devoured the longhorn.

The moon began its slow ascent.

Finally, its appetite sated, the thing wandered back into the woods that surrounded Patty Ferguson's new farm.

ALAN AND BILLY HURRIED up the steps, and went into the house.

Phoebe had picked up Derek and Catharine. They were in the living room, playing an elaborate hide-and-seek game with Little Bit.

Phoebe kissed Billy, and Katie kissed Alan.

"Okay, we're here," said Alan. "What's going on?"

Katie said, "Come to the kitchen."

Carol Grace and Mary were sitting in the floor beside the China cabinet, leaning against the wall.

"Ask them."

"Hi, Alan," said Carol Grace.

"Hi, Billy," said Mary.

Billy crossed his arms. "Okay, girls, what have you done?"

Both girls looked at the floor.

"We went out behind the barn," said Carol Grace.

"And we took each other's hand," added Mary.

"We were allowed to ask our own questions."

"And we were allowed to remember it all."

Alan couldn't find it in himself to admonish the girls for doing what, for them, came naturally.

Billy seemed to thaw after a moment, too.

Alan was the first to speak. "And you asked...?"

Carol Grace spoke up. "We asked about Madeline...and why she means so much right now."

"But we were told that we couldn't tell anyone," said Mary.

Both Alan and Billy looked at Gabriel for confirmation. He nodded.

Carol Grace continued. "Then we asked some other stuff..."

"We asked how Pam fits into all of this."

"But we can't tell any of you that, either."

"Then we asked some other stuff..."

Both girls turned beet red.

Billy smiled. "Boys?"

Mary smiled an embarrassed smile, and nodded. "Finally, we asked about the asuwang."

"We knew that both of you were really worried about it...and about it killing people," said Carol Grace.

"We were told how to find it, and how to kill it."

"We were also told that it's pregnant. If you don't hurry, you'll have to kill two of them."

Both men goggled at the girls.

Margo Sardis cackled with laughter at the sight. Soon, Katie, Phoebe, and Pam joined in. Even Gabriel smiled at the looks on the men's faces.

Alan said, "After all this death, the answer was so simple...and right in front of us!"

Billy said, "Okay, so how do kill it?"

Carol Grace pointed to Gabriel. "He has access to a sword that will cut its head off."

The two lawmen looked at the angel with eyebrows raised.

Gabriel looked at the girls, amazement showing in his eyes. "What sword?"

"The Sword of the Spirit," said Mary.

Gabriel's eyes widened. "Seriously?"

Both girls nodded.

Gabriel turned to Alan and Billy. "Yes, I have access to it, and I can let you use it. I'm just amazed that the girls were told about it." He closed his eyes and focused. Suddenly, into his hand, a sword and scabbard appeared. A metal belt ran through the scabbard's slits. Gabriel opened his eyes and looked at the sword. It glowed with a faint white power. He turned to the lawmen. "This is His very sword, made from His word. Nothing evil can stand before it. Only one of you may use it." Gabriel passed it to Alan.

Alan showed concern. "Me? Why me?"

"I don't know. I also don't question. This is a great gift, Alan...and a great honor. It shows that your faith never wavers."

Alan gently took the sword from Gabriel. "Now all we need to do is find the asuwang."

Billy looked at the two girls. "And how do we do that?"

"You have to see it in a mirror," said Mary.

"The reflection always shows its true self," added Carol Grace.

"And we were told how to lure it out into the open."

Alan said, "And how do we do that?"

The girls told them.

"That just might work, Alan," said Billy.

"We'll have to bring Tory in on the secret."

The two men began discussing strategies.

Katie, exasperation in voice, said, "That's *it*?"

Alan turned around, puzzled. His face cleared up. "Oh, yeah! Thank you, girls! This is a big help!"

"You're kidding, right?" asked Katie.

The two lawmen looked at Katie, eyebrows raised.

"What's wrong, Katie?" asked Billy.

Katie gestured at Carol Grace and Mary. "You aren't going to say anything to them about joining hands *on their own?* It could have been dangerous!"

"But, Katie, nothing happened...," Billy began.

"Honey, they only did what comes naturally," added Alan, giving voice to his earlier thought.

"*That isn't the point!*"

"Child," said Margo.

Katie seemed not to hear her aunt. "They could have...oh, I don't know...gotten hurt or something!"

"*Child!*"

Katie turned to Margo.

"Stop," Margo said simply. "Alan is right...*and you know it.*"

"But, Aunt Margo..."

Margo held up a finger. "No buts, Katie. How will these girls learn to contain their powers if they don't use them enough to gain experience?"

Phoebe stood up. "Katie, I usually agree with you, but, this time, I have to agree with Margo." She walked over to Katie, and placed her hand on Katie's shoulder. "We can't protect them forever. And they've shown that they're very able to take care of themselves."

Katie's shoulders slumped in defeat. "I know. I just want to protect them."

"Child, come here." Margo had also stood.

Katie went to her aunt. Margo folded her into a hug.

"Katie, we have to let them learn...and we have to let them try out their wings. It's natural," said Margo.

Katie hugged back. "I know, Auntie. It's just so hard."

After a moment, Katie broke the hug. She turned to Billy and Alan. "I'm sorry." To Carol Grace and Mary, she said, "I'm sorry for freaking out, girls."

Carol Grace smiled. "It's okay, Mom. I love you, too."

Katie took a deep breath. "Phoebe, want to help me finish dinner?" She held her hand out to her best friend.

Phoebe smiled. "Of course, Katie." Phoebe reached out and took Katie's hand.

A huge bright flash of bluish-white light burst from the two women's clasped hands and encapsulated them, forming a round bubble. A loud *BOOM*, felt rather than heard, shook the house. Dishes fell from the China cabinet and shattered as they hit the floor beside Mary and Carol Grace. Both women's heads were thrown back, and their eyes rolled back into their heads until only the whites could be seen. They lifted until they were three feet off of the ground.

Everyone's eyes were on the two women. Billy's eyes were wide in disbelief. Alan was shocked.

"Is that what *we* look like?" asked Carol Grace.

"Awww, *shit*! Not them *too*," said Alan.

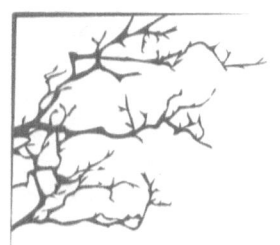

Chapter 11

Tory had overseen the landing of not one, but *two* FBI helicopters behind the Perry City Hall. Mayor Tepes stood with Tory during the landing.

Tory could have sworn that the Mayor's eyes had a deeply red tint, but he dismissed it as a reflection of the parking lot's lights.

As the rotors slowed to a stop, each helicopter disgorged several people. Tory met them, told them where the crime scene could be found, and gave the lead forensic person his cell phone number. He recommended Ethel's Diner if anyone got hungry.

After the briefing, Tory did the best thing a smart investigator could do: he left the team to work its own scientific magic.

Jim and the Justice Security crew had waited for him. Waiting with them was Mary and Adam – Jim had dispatched Emily to pick them up. Tory walked over to them.

"Everyone ready?" asked Tory, after he had kissed his wife and son.

"We're as ready as we can be, I guess," answered Jim. He smiled his hundred-watt smile at Tory. Sparkles reflected in his smile from the surrounding lights.

Tory laughed at the sight. "Then, let's load up and head to Junior's Farm!"

Three cars pulled into the long driveway at the farm. They parked side-by-side and climbed the steps to the porch. Patty knocked on the door.

A little boy, around seven, opened the door.

Patty grinned at him. "Hi! I'm Patty, and these are my friends. Alan invited us to dinner. May we come in?"

The boy turned his head and yelled into the kitchen. "Alan! Patty and her friends are here!"

"Tell them to come in, Derek!" came the answer.

"You can come in now," Derek said to Patty.

The group went into the house, and headed for the kitchen.

They all drew up and stopped at the wide kitchen doorway. They stared at the force bubble that contained Katie and Phoebe.

"Hol-eee shit!" said Brandon.

"What the *hell* is this?" said Jim.

Alan shook his head with amusement. "Just another fun day full of magic at Junior's Farm."

"Alan, I thought you said that it was the two girls that did this!" said Patty.

"I did. This is something new."

"Oh, my God," said Mary Masterson. "It's all true, isn't it?"

"Oh, yeah," said Billy. "It's all true, all right."

Everyone stared at the two women for a moment.

"So, is this all that they do?" asked Tory.

"I don't know," answered Alan. "This happened just before you got here."

Margo Sardis, forgotten in the corner of the kitchen, was stumped. "I'm amazed by this."

"Why, Aunt Margo?" replied Alan. "We've all seen what happened with the girls."

Margo shook her head. "This is different."

Pam looked at Margo. "Different *how*, Miss Margo?"

"Baby, I'm *your* aunt, too, apparently. At least, according to Gabriel here." She shook her head again. "I can understand the girls. One is pure Sardis, the other is half Sardis and half angel." She gestured with her cane toward the two women floating three feet off the ground. "*This* is pure Sardis magic. No angels involved."

"*Angels*?" said Jim. "What happened here? Are we missing something?"

"Oh. Sorry," said Alan. He gestured to Gabriel. "Justice Security folks, this is Gabriel. He's the father of Phoebe's kids. Also, please note the trumpet hanging from his belt loop." He paused for a couple of beats. "He's *the* Gabriel. Angel."

Tory looked at Jim. "What in Hell have you people gotten us into?"

Emily responded to Tory's comment. "I think Joey Justice would argue with you about being in Hell."

Mary Masterson said, "Tory, behave yourself. You have to believe in the good, and fight the evil."

Tory gestured to the two floating women. "And which is this, Mary?"

Gabriel said quietly, "It's good, Tory. You have no reason to disparage these two fine women simply because you're frightened."

Tory started to retort. He held it inside once he realized that Gabriel was correct.

"*PATTY FERGUSON,*" said a voice from inside the bubble.

Patty's face drained all of its color. "Y-y-yes?"

"*A HELLBEAST HAS FED ON ONE OF YOUR PETS. THE SARDIS WITCHES WILL NOW CAST A PROTECTION SPELL FOR YOUR FARM. IT WILL PREVENT HARM COMING TO ANYONE OR ANYTHING ON YOUR PROPERTY. THIS SPELL WILL NOT NEED TO BE RECAST.*"

Neither woman inside the bubble moved their lips, but both had their mouths open. After the pronouncement, a bluish-white sphere exited the bubble, trailing a tail of bluish-white energy behind it.

All eyes were on the sphere as it left the kitchen. It flew into the living room. At the front door, it passed through easily and sped out of sight.

Margo Sardis was the first to break the silence. "That must be a very powerful spell. The best I can do is a couple of days, but this one doesn't need to be recast." Her eyes turned to her nieces inside the bubble. "*Strong* magic."

"Th-thank you," murmured Patty. "I have to go. Brandon, will you come with me?"

"*NO ONE MAY LEAVE THE SARDIS FARM UNTIL ALL PROTECTION SPELLS ARE IN PLACE.*"

Alan looked at his wife and Phoebe as they hung in the air. "Well. Doesn't that twitch your broomstick?"

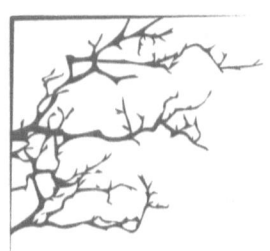

Chapter 12

Cliff Anderson locked the front door of the real estate office. His mind was on all of the business that he'd done in the last couple of days.

The Justice Security people were becoming even better sources of business than the people from the big box store had been. Jim Dandy had told Cliff that people would be drifting in for the next couple of months, and that many would only be renting at first. Several would be residents of the new building going up close to Junior's Farm, but most would be living in the community. Jim, Patty, Tory, and Emily would be recommending Anderson's Realty And Auction (*Sardis County's BEST!*) to all of their relocating employees.

Cliff had truly been blessed by these people. And he was delighted that, as of right now, he had plenty of real estate options available.

Today, Cliff had sold two more properties – one in Perry, and one in London. The London property had been handled from start to finish by Arlene, since Cliff's other employees were showing rental properties to more Justice Security people.

"Arlene, I can't thank you enough," Cliff had told his secretary. "I'll happily give you full commission on the sale...might start doing that anyway. I don't know why I haven't started letting you do some selling as it is."

Arlene had met Cliff's eyes and smiled broadly. "Thank you, Cliff. You're a great guy, and not just because of this."

Cliff blushed. It wasn't because of the compliment, but because a picture of Arlene's beautiful legs wrapped around his waist went through his mind again. "You're welcome, Arlene," he replied.

Arlene moved close to Cliff. Very close. So close that should either of them chosen to kiss the other, very little movement would be required to make it happen.

"Someday, Cliff, we're going to have to work on your fear of London," whispered Arlene. She was looking directly into Cliff's eyes. "I think I can help you get over it. No, I'm *sure* of it."

Cliff, as frightened of London as he was, said, "Maybe you can, Arlene. We'll have to try it sometime."

Arlene put the palm of her hand on Cliff's chest, directly over his heart. "Yes, we will. Soon." She kissed Cliff's cheek.

Cliff stood with his mouth open and his eyes wide as Arlene had walked away from him.

Now, alone at the end of the day, standing under the streetlight that shone in the darkness in front of the real estate office that bore his name, Cliff Anderson was kicking himself for not following up on Arlene's offer.

Clifford, you *are a dumbass. A straight-up, dyed-in-the-wool dumbass. The woman of your dreams* kissed *you, and you just stood there!* Cliff shook his head as these thoughts ran through his head. *She likes you. It won't get any plainer than that!*

"Hello, Cliff," said a voice from the darkness.

Cliff froze, startled. He looked around, trying to see who had spoken, but the streetlight made the darkness even darker. "Who...who's there? Do I know you? Who are you?"

The voice seemed to be smiling as it replied. "I'm your boogie man, Cliff."

"My...my boogie man? Huh?"

Cliff caught a glimpse of a figure moving just outside of the streetlight's downward glow.

"I really don't want to feed again so soon, but, then again, I've never been pregnant before, either," said the voice.

Realization hit Cliff, and his blood turned to ice. "You're the Slasher, aren't you?"

The voice chuckled. "That's what they call me. You know me by another name."

Cliff was poised between fight and flee. He wasn't sure either choice would do any good.

A loud growl came from the left of the real estate office. Cliff whirled. When he saw what was there, he couldn't believe his eyes.

Padding slowly and gracefully into the light was the largest wolf Cliff had ever seen. Of course, he hadn't seen many outside of zoos, anyway, but this wolf was huge. If it had stood upright, it would have been almost tall enough to look into his eyes.

The wolf's eyes were fixed on whoever was outside the circle of light. The wolf snarled, and began uttering a low growl.

Cliff felt his hackles rise. His eyes widened as a thought struck him. *They're rising just like when I go to...*

Stiff-legged, the wolf continued to growl.

The voice in the darkness hissed, "*Get Away! The prey is* MINE*!*"

The wolf crouched on its haunches, preparing to leap. Its growl became an intense warning.

The voice in the darkness hissed again.

Cliff watched with fascination. *The wolf is protecting me!*

The wolf sprang at the figure.

Cliff couldn't see what was happening, but it sounded as if it was an intense fight.

Two other wolves bounded past Cliff toward the melee in the dark.

The figure in the darkness hissed again, then continued a loud keening that grew fainter...as if it were running away.

The growling from the wolves also grew fainter. They were in pursuit.

But not all of them.

The first wolf again padded gracefully into the light. It met Cliff's eyes.

Cliff, now unafraid, looked into the wolf's eyes.

Arlene? Cliff shook his head. *Now what made me think that?*

The wolf sat in front of Cliff, at his feet. It held Cliff's gaze.

"Th-thank you," Cliff said to the wolf.

The wolf, with grace and great care, stood on its hind legs, and placed its front paws on each of Cliff's shoulders.

Cliff, still unafraid, continued to gaze into the wolf's eyes.

The wolf gently placed one paw on Cliff's chest, and gently licked Cliff's cheek...the same cheek that Arlene had kissed earlier that day.

"I'm so in love with you, Arlene, that there aren't words to express it."

The wolf seemed to grin. Then it abruptly turned and ran into the darkness from which it came.

Now, why did I tell that to a wolf?

INJURED! OH INJURED! Is baby hurt? Injured! Wolfses injured!

The asuwang had reached its dwelling, and was safe behind its doors. It was breathing deeply and sporadically.

A loud *THUMP* came from the dwelling door as one of the wolves threw itself at it.

Not coming in not coming in! Too thick for you, wolfses! Can't injure more! Go away!

The asuwang huddled with its injuries...and its hunger.

BILLY SAID, "MS. MARGO, how about reaching in and pulling those two out?"

Margo snorted. "You're kidding, right? There's no way I'm doing that! I might get sucked into it, too!"

Tory turned to Mary. "Honey, I'm sorry."

Mary Masterson looked at her husband. "Sorry? For what?"

Tory gestured widely. "For getting you into all of this!"

"Tory!" Mary sounded exasperated. "Stop it! This is the best fun ever!"

Tory stared at his wife with wide eyes. He wasn't quite sure that he'd heard her properly.

Billy's cell phone rang. "Napier."

"Sheriff, this is Cliff Anderson. I think I was next in line to be the Slasher's next victim."

"What makes you think that, Cliff?"

"Someone was waiting for me to leave the office tonight. It was too dark to see them, but I could hear them, all right. He...or she, I couldn't tell...said, 'Hello, Cliff. I'm your boogie man', or something like that, anyway."

Heads turned to look at Billy as he loudly said, "How the hell did you get away from him?"

"I'd...I'd rather explain that to you in person, Sheriff."

"Right. Where are you?"

"My office."

"Good. I'll be there as soon as I can." Billy hung up, and put the phone into his pocket. He looked up at Phoebe and Katie. "I know you think that it's important that I stay here, but I need to get out. I have a monster to catch. Please."

"What happened, Billy?" asked Alan.

"The asuwang almost got Cliff Anderson. He escaped somehow...won't tell me over the phone."

Tory let out a low whistle. "Did he get a look at it?"

"No."

Carol Grace and Mary Smalls were watching their mothers. The two women floated silently, with their heads thrown back and their eyes white.

No one was watching the girls. They turned their attention to Pam.

Pam caught their eyes. After a moment, she nodded. She stood, and quietly walked to her sister and cousin. The three girls walked to their mothers.

Derek and Catherine were watching their older sisters and their cousin.

Jim Dandy was speaking. "We have to hope that the FBI people come up with a lead. I'm at a loss as to what else to do."

Carol Grace, Mary, and Pam nodded to each other. Carol Grace reached for Katie, and Mary Smalls reached for Phoebe. Once they had their mothers' free hand, they reached for Pam's hands.

Gabriel watched quietly, a slight smile playing around his lips.

Margo saw what was happening, and tried to stop it. "*NO, GIRLS! DON'T DO IT!*"

Everyone turned just as Pam's hands caught the girls' and completed the circuit.

The world turned white.

CLIFF SAT AT HIS DESK, waiting for the Sheriff to arrive.

What did I just see? What just saved me out there?

He shook his head in disbelief.

I've never heard of wolves acting that way.

He smiled slightly. *And why did I immediately think of Arlene?*

A sound came to him. It was the sound of a key turning in the front door. Cliff turned toward the door.

Arlene walked through, turned, and locked the door behind her.

Cliff rose from his desk as Arlene turned toward him.

Their eyes met.

"That was you out there, wasn't it?"

Arlene smiled broadly. "Out where, Cliff?"

Cliff gestured toward the front door. "Outside! The Slasher was here! Wolves chased it away!"

"Wolves, Cliff?"

Cliff spluttered, and finally just stopped trying to talk. "Did I imagine them?" He slumped down into his chair. "Maybe I did."

Arlene walked over to him and smoothed his hair. She bent down low and whispered into his ear.

"I love you, too, Cliff."

THE KITCHEN OF JUNIOR'S Farm glowed white with power. It was blinding.

The two Sardis mothers and the three Sardis daughters floated three feet from the ground. The white glow came from the power emanating from them. It came from their eyes, their open mouths, their noses, and their ears.

Margo goggled at them with everyone else. She was astounded at the raw power displayed by the five females. *How much more powerful would it be if I had joined?*

Margo looked at Gabe. He was smiling.

"It's not too late, Margo," he told her. "You can still join your power to theirs."

Margo slowly shook her head. "No. Not until I have to. If it becomes a matter of life and death."

"Oh, my God," said Alan. "Somebody tell me what we're seeing. Please."

Derek and Catherine watched with broad smiles on their faces, as if they knew that their times were coming.

Patty, Brandon, Jim, Emily, and the Mastersons had all slid to the floor, and sat. They watched with wonder in their eyes.

Tory and Mary Masterson crossed themselves.

Sheriff Billy Napier saw it all. Finally, he decided that he had had enough.

"That's *it!* I see all of this power, I hear all of these prophecies, and I watch things that could make normal people insane...*and none of it helps me find this damn asuwang!*" Billy took a step forward, toward the floating women. "So, unless you can help me stop the killer, *let me out of this damn house!*"

The voice, rather than being heard from everywhere, spoke inside the heads of all that were present.

"Patience, Billy Napier. You are a good man, and we will help you," said the voice.

Everyone was confused. Was it the voice of the women, or the voice of the power supporting the women?

Each of the floating five jerked their heads slightly in the same direction. A bolt of pure white power came into existence, and took off through the front door.

"You and Alan must follow the light. It will brighten the dwelling of the asuwang, and will follow the asuwang wherever it goes. Watch for the wolves. They have attacked the beast, and guard it even now. They will help you. Take the Sword Of The Spirit. Go now."

With that pronouncement, the five witches floated to the floor of the kitchen. The blinding white glow faded, and each witch returned to themselves.

Each of them had a dazed look.

Billy and Alan each rushed to the sides of their wives and children. Amid assurances that all were okay, just tired, "We're fine! Really!", Alan walked to the China cabinet, reached to the top, and pulled down the sword. He examined it, and belted it on.

"Let's go, Billy. Time to kill an asuwang," said Alan.

Billy nodded his agreement, and the two men left.

THE ASUWANG PEEKED out a window.

Seven wolves now patrolled the dwelling.

The asuwang hissed at the wolves.

"Go away, wolfses! Leave me be!"

The wolves either didn't hear, or chose to ignore the asuwang.

The asuwang had lost control of its body-shaping properties, and began changing between human form and its natural form.

It desperately hissed at the wolves again as it looked out the window.

One of the wolves howled. It was loud and long.

The asuwang noticed a bright, white ball flying through the sky to its dwelling. Wide-eyes, it watched the ball hover directly over its dwelling. The ball began glowing even brighter, making the night almost as bright as the day.

The asuwang released another panicked hiss.

BILLY AND ALAN DROVE along the road between Junior's Farm and Perry.

Alan pointed. "There goes the spell!!

Billy, cut his eyes toward the fireball and the tail, and nodded. "You keep an eye on where it goes, and I'll drive."

The patrol car's lights and siren were on, and Billy drove fast in order to catch up with the white fireball.

"It's heading for town," said Alan.

Billy nodded. He had a grim look on his face. "Probably lives right in the middle of us."

As the two lawmen arrived at the Perry city limits, the fireball began arcing down.

"Looks like it's heading for Bailey Avenue," said Alan. "I can't say for sure, though."

"Let's kill the siren and roll down our windows. Maybe we can hear something that will help," said Billy.

Alan turned off the siren, and both men rolled down their windows as they traversed the residential sections of Perry.

They both heard a wolf howl.

The men shared a brief look between them.

Suddenly, the night sky became almost bright as day.

Billy stopped the car as Alan pointed. Neither man said a word for a moment.

The fireball hovered over a normal-looking house in the middle of Bailey Avenue. Several wolves patrolled around the house, and one sat on the house's front sidewalk. It chose that moment to lift its head and howl again.

"Alan. That's Ted Baker's house."

"OH, MY GOD!" SAID EMILY.

Everyone turned toward Emily. She pointed to the five Sardis witches.

Katie, Carol Grace, Phoebe, Pam, and Mary looked different. Each of them now had hair that had turned completely white.

Margo Sardis eyed her nieces. "Looks like all that power is making its mark on you."

Katie pulled some of her hair around so that she could see it. "White. Not grey. Not silver." She released her hair and looked around the room. "Why? And why the girls? They're only thirteen!"

Carol Grace looked into the mirrored back of the China cabinet. "Oh. Em. Gee! This is so *cool!*"

Mary came to her side. "We look *killer* with this white hair!"

Jim Dandy made a face. "Bad choice of words, girls." To Katie, he said, "Ms. Blake, thank you for your hospitality, but I believe it's time for all of us to go. Patty wants to check on her farm, and Tory wants to get his family home. Perhaps we can all get together another time?" Jim flashed a hundred-watt-smile at Katie. The kitchen light twinkled in his teeth.

Katie turned to them. "Of course! I'm so sorry about all of this! Please do come back, will you?"

Jim smiled. "You bet we will."

Mary Masterson took Katie's hand. "You've been so kind. If I can help in any way, please don't hesitate to ask." Adam, cradled in his mother's arms, smiled at Katie.

"Thank you all. We will get together again soon, I promise," replied Katie.

The Mastersons left with the Justice Security people.

After they had closed the door behind them, Phoebe collapsed into a kitchen chair and began crying. "What does all this mean?"

Mary and Pam went to their mother and wrapped her in their arms.

"Mom," said Pam, "it's going to be okay. We're witches. No, we're *Sardis* witches...and nothing can beat that!"

Carol Grace and Katie joined in the group hug, and shared their belief in that as well.

Gabriel, who had remained quiet during all of this, said, "I hate to be the bearer of bad news...or good news...depends on how you look at it, I guess. But you still have one more Sardis and one more half angel to add to the mix. Once that's done, Hell doesn't stand a chance!"

THE ASUWANG SAW THE sheriff's patrol car parked outside its house. Its panic reached a new level, and with the panic, came the first hint that a birth would be happening soon...maybe tonight.

Wolfses brought the witches...witches brought the sheriff. Gotta run...gotta go...

It looked out the window. The sheriff and the deputy were walking toward the front walk. The wolf stood, wagged its tail, and bowed its head in deference once.

The asuwang looked at the deputy, and saw what it was carrying.

Sword of the Spirit! Gotta run! Gotta go NOW!

It sprinted for the back door.

"THE WOMEN SAID THAT the wolves would help us, right?" asked Alan.

Billy nodded as he climbed out of the car. "Yep. I'm not even going to ask where the wolves came from."

Alan laughed a short, nervous laugh as he came to Billy's side. "Well, this *is* Sardis County."

"Right."

They crossed the street. The wolf on the sidewalk watched them come.

Billy spoke to the wolf. "Thank you for your help."

The wolf stood, wagged its tail, and bowed its head in acknowledgement.

Alan drew the Sword of the Spirit.

The two men arrived at the front door of the house.

"I'd like you wolves to back us up, please," said Billy.

The wolf chuffed its response.

"If it gets away from us, track it. We'll follow."

The wolf met the sheriff's eyes. Billy could have sworn it was thinking, *Well, gee, what else do you think we'd do?*

Billy smiled. "Okay, I know, I just want to keep everyone on the same page." *I'm talking to a wolf as if it can understand me. But it* does *understand me. I don't want to think about why.*

Billy pounded on the front door. "Ted! Ted Baker! Open up! It's Billy!"

Silence from inside the house.

Billy and Alan shared a look. Billy backed up to kick the door, as Alan poised the sword for a killing blow.

Before the kick could be delivered, a howl came from the back of the house, then two more.

The wolf that stood with the sheriff looked toward the back with ears raised. Then it turned to Billy.

"Let's go! Don't wait for us!" said Billy.

The three took off after the others. The wolf quickly outpaced the two lawmen.

The fireball over the house began trailing into town, following the asuwang.

TED BAKER'S HOUSE WAS only two streets over from the Court Square in Perry.

The asuwang fled toward town, not knowing if it should go to the Medical Examiner's office, the Sardis County Sentinel Press offices, or the Sheriff's Office.

The wolves were hot on its trail.

The witches' fireball was almost overhead.

The asuwang turned toward the Sheriff's Office. Perhaps it could hide in the darkness of the jail cells.

STEVE BELL, THE ONLY person on duty in the Sheriff's Office, stepped outside to look at the fireball. He had never seen anything like it.

There were currently no prisoners in the jail. Two deputies were on patrol, and dispatching was handled by the Perry Police Department. Steve was basically a babysitter, in case someone was arrested.

Steve stepped out to the parking lot to get a closer view of the fireball. It was heading straight for the Sheriff's Office!

Steve saw Ted Baker duck inside the Sheriff's Office. The door slammed shut.

The fireball stopped directly over the building. It glowed brightly, almost as bright as day.

Steve saw several wolves run to the front of the Sheriff's Office. They stopped at the door. Then they began circling the building.

One more wolf arrived, and sat a few feet away from the door.

Steve saw Billy and Alan run to the door and slam into the Sheriff's Office. Alan had been carrying a sword that glowed slightly. The single wolf followed them in.

Steve decided that this would be a good time for a cup of coffee and a piece of pie from Ethel's.

ON THE MAIN HIGHWAY, a nondescript sedan with three passengers had just passed the sign that read, "*Welcome To Sardis County! Where* YOU *Make The Magic!*" Underneath that, the sign read, "*A Nice Place To Live!*"

"Not long now," the driver said to the two passengers.

"That's, you know, great! I gotta, you know, piss like a racehorse, you know?" replied one of the passengers.

"I told you to hold off on the coffee," said the other passenger.

The driver shook his head and smiled to himself. *They've been picking on each other for six hours straight. They'll fit right in with the rest of us!*

"TED!" CALLED BILLY. "Ted, the party's over. Come on out and pay the piper!"

Silence answered him.

"Honestly, Billy, would *you* come out to face certain death?" asked Alan.

Billy smiled at his old friend. "No, I guess not."

The wolf, nose to the floor, walked to the door that separated the jail cells from the offices. It snorted, pawed the door, and looked back at the two men. *He's in here, guys...what's the holdup?*

"Billy?"

"Yeah?"

"I guess I should go first, since I have the only thing that will kill it."

"I guess so."

Alan held the sword ready, and moved to the door. The wolf moved out of the way, but remained close. "Here we go." He reached out and opened the door.

The wolf moved past his legs and took the lead. Alan followed, and Billy brought up the rear. As they entered the hallway, Billy closed the door behind them and used the key to lock the deadbolt.

"Nobody's leaving. It's us or that thing," said Billy.

A hiss came from the jail cells.

The wolf's ears came up, and it loped down the hall, growling.

Alan and Billy followed close behind.

"You just couldn't leave me alone, could you?" said a voice from the darkness. "I came here a few months ago, thinking this would be a great place to raise a little one. I had no idea how wrong I was!"

Billy said, "A few months ago? Then you aren't really Ted Baker! What happened to him?"

A low chuckle. "He was my first meal here. I had to stash him in the crawlspace under his house."

"WOW! SOMEBODY MUST have been watching Mayberry reruns when they built this town!" said the driver.

"Hey! What's that, you know, fireball over that, you know, that building?" said the first passenger.

"And check out the wolves," said the second passenger.

The sedan had turned onto the Court Square. They stopped in the parking lot of the Sheriff's Office.

"Let's check it out," said the driver.

WITH AN ABRUPT GROWL, the wolf sprang at the asuwang with its teeth bared.

The asuwang batted it away with one arm and hissed at the two lawmen.

Billy feinted to the right, and the wolf sprang again, also from the right of the monster. The monster focused its attention on Billy and the wolf.

Quickly, Alan swung the Sword Of The Spirit with as much strength as he could muster. With a blinding white flash, the blade severed the asuwang's head. The body collapsed, and the head rolled underneath the bunk in the open jail cell behind it.

The two lawmen breathed heavily, and the wolf panted.

From under the bunk, something hissed at them.

The three turned.

Billy said, "I'll shine the light. You be ready with that sword."

As the three looked under the bunk, the light caught the eyes of a smaller version of the headless asuwang.

It had given birth.

"Aww, crap," said Billy. He looked at the wolf. "Who's gonna drag it out of there so that Alan can kill it?"

THE THREE MEN ENTERED the Sheriff's Office. They saw no one.

At a nod from the driver, all three drew handguns, and held them at the ready.

A click came from the door to the cellblock hallway. The three men turned their weapons toward the sound.

The door opened, and two lawmen and a wolf came through. The sheriff was carrying two heads, each with an elongated snout, sharp teeth, and foot-long tongues sticking out of the snouts. One head was much smaller than the other.

The wolf drew up short. The two lawmen saw the three men, held up the heads, and said, "Hello, gents. I'm Sheriff Napier. Know anything about asuwangs?"

The three men, sensing that the danger was over, put away their weapons.

"Hi, Sheriff," said the driver. He pointed to the first passenger. "That's Snickers." He pointed to the second passenger. "That's Nicholas Turner. I'm Joey Justice. We don't know squat about asuwangs, but Nicky and I have been to Hell and back."

"Snickers it is." Joey smiled. "You, Jim, and Nicholas need to start work on the computer system. Patty, Brandon, I'd like you guys to start working with the people that are trickling in. Get them trained and ready for anything." He shook his head. "Wow. Now we not only have to worry about Esteban Fernandez, but we're getting caught up in magical problems, too." He smiled. "But, I guess it's just another day in Sardis County, right?"

About The Author: T. M. Bilderback is a former radio announcer with a number of story ideas running around inside his head, most based on or inspired by classic songs. The author currently resides in Tennessee, and is writing feverishly in order to banish these stories from his head and into book form before he runs screaming into the street.

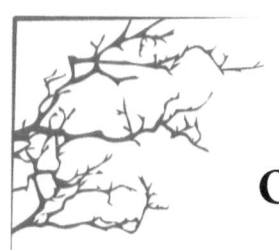

Other works by T. M. Bilderback

N<u>**icholas Turner**</u>
    If You Could Read My Mind
<u>**Justice Security**</u>
Mama Told Me Not To Come
Someone Saved My Life Tonight
Jackie Blue
Wake Me Up Before You Go-Go
Saturday In The Park
MacArthur Park
The Little Drummer Boy
The Night Chicago Died
Jim Dandy
Cow Patty
Hell's Bells
<u>**Tales Of Sardis County**</u>
Don't Come Around Here No More
Junior's Farm
The Devil's In The Details
I'm Your Boogie Man
<u>**Colonel Abernathy's Tales**</u>
The Lion Sleeps Tonight
Heart Of Glass
<u>**Other Stories**</u>
The Wreck Of The Edmund Fitzgerald
Gold
Hot Child In The City
Eli's Coming
<u>**Other Novels**</u>
Empty Eyes
<u>**Short Story Collections**</u>
Greatest Hits

Don't miss out!

Visit the website below and you can sign up to receive emails whenever T. M. Bilderback publishes a new book. There's no charge and no obligation.

https://books2read.com/r/B-A-KAW-ROIY

BOOKS 2 READ

Connecting independent readers to independent writers.